A Bitter Magic

A Bitter Magic

RODERICK TOWNLEY

ALFRED A. KNOPF
NEW YORK

THIS IS A BORZOI BOOK PUBLISHED BY ALFRED A. KNOPF

Visit us on the Web! randomhousekids.com

Educators and librarians, for a variety of teaching tools, visit us at RHTeachersLibrarians.com

Library of Congress Cataloging-in-Publication Data
Townley, Rod.
A bitter magic / Roderick Townley. — First edition.
p. cm.
Summary: When twelve-year-old Cisley's mother, who controls real magic, disappears during a magic act, Cisley is left with her cold, distant uncle and a great mystery which will only be solved if she can summon her own magic.
ISBN 978-0-449-81649-3 (trade) — ISBN 978-0-449-81650-9 (lib. bdg.) — ISBN 978-0-449-81651-6 (ebook)
[1. Magic—Fiction. 2. Missing persons—Fiction. 3. Mothers and daughters—Fiction. 4. Uncles—Fiction. 5. Mystery and detective stories.] I. Title.
PZ7.T64965Bi 2015 [Fic]—dc23 2014013601

The text of this book is set in 11.5-point Dutch 823.

Printed in the United States of America
November 2015
10 9 8 7 6 5 4 3 2 1

First Edition

For Wyatt
sharing the mirror

Contents

PART ONE

Thirty Feet of Wind

Chapter One

Her eyes had that special glint they get when she's about to do something she shouldn't. I've learned to be careful with Mother. Not argue. Just be careful.

It was her idea to put me in the audience—way up in the balcony—instead of backstage, where I could be useful. My only problem is sitting still in this dress with the ridiculous ribbons that tickle my neck. Does she think I'm still a little girl?

Look at those fancy ladies down there, and the stiff-backed men beside them with medals on their chests and wax on their curled mustaches. They have no idea what goes into a show like ours.

We don't want them to, of course.

The sea starts moving. Waves of evening gowns rise. Applause surges through the hall.

"Cisley!" Miss Porlock hisses. "Stand up! He's coming!"

"Who?"

My tutor nods meaningfully at the box seats. After a moment, the great man himself—the archduke—ducks his head and steps in, a severely thin person with thick eyebrows. Beside him stand two armed attendants and a woman in an enormous gown. I can guess what they're thinking: *Amuse us, peasants.*

The audience subsides into their seats, lights dim, and Uncle Asa bounds to center stage. I have to admit he looks snappy with his slicked-back hair, pointy beard, and toothpick-thin mustache. He bows and makes his little speech. It's his show after all: the Amazing Thummel, Illusionist, & Co.

Mother and I are the *& Co.*

Then comes the part I can never understand, as many times as I've seen it. It kind of drives me crazy. The theater goes dark, and tiny points of light float out over the audience. Mother once told me they were "elementals," whatever that means. Now hundreds drift through the hall, glimmering dimly. Even the know-it-alls let out an "Aah," as if a swarm of fairies has filtered among them.

Onstage, a single spotlight comes up, and there stands Mother, looking— Well, a German newspaper once called Marina Thummel the most beautiful woman in Europe. I couldn't tell you; I've seen her in too many ugly moods. But just now, in her ice-blue gown, she looks out over the audience with that secret not-quite smile of hers that makes grown men squirm. It's true. I've seen it happen.

I glance down at my hands, struck again by the awful truth: I'll never have that effect on anyone.

Mother holds open a beaded purse. She makes a gesture to the floating lights, and they begin circling toward her, then around her. Finally they enter the purse, which she snaps shut with a triumphant smile. Her look says, "Wouldn't you like to know how I did that!"

The audience breaks out of its trance to applaud wildly. I applaud, too. Proud and embarrassed. You'd be, too, if it was your mother up there.

The trick is her secret. She won't tell anyone, including Uncle Asa, how she does it. "Magic," she snapped at him during one of their spats, "is not a recipe. It's a *talent*. One you'll never have."

Next comes the part I'm usually in; but Mother said tonight she'd let Benny, the stagehand's young son, fill in.

"But he's only eight!"

"Cisley, dear," she cooed. She was staring into the vanity mirror, applying mascara at the corners of her eyes. "You were eight when you started."

It's true. But I was good at it. Luckily, this particular trick is simple: just stand there with your arms out, and rise into the air.

Sure enough, up he goes, a foolish little boy floating a dozen feet over the stage.

It makes me wince to see Benny grinning and flapping his arms as if he's done some great thing. In fact, of course, he's done nothing at all. Never left the ground. Uncle Asa's mirrors do everything, tilting his image upward, swerving him from side to side, and setting him down again.

Miss Porlock shoots me a look. For those who don't know her, that look can seem fierce—forehead bulging and mouth turned down—but it's simply the face God gave her. Dear, clumsy Miss Porlock, a danger at any tea party, but kind. She's a relative, I'm told, a distant cousin or something.

"I like it when *you* do it," Miss P. whispers, and pats my knee.

The show goes on, and I wonder again why Mother wanted me out front. "Something special," she said, with a white-gloved finger to her lips and her eyes bright as emeralds. "Don't say anything to your uncle."

I have that grumbly feeling in my stomach again. I always get it when I'm nervous, which is a good part of the time, now that I think of it. I glance over at Miss Porlock and am surprised to see her gnawing her lip. Then I hear an undertone coming from her and realize she's muttering. She does that when she gets emotional. It's kind of embarrassing.

"You can tell me," I whisper during the disappearing-cabinet act. "What's going on?"

"Whatever do you mean?"

I just keep looking at her.

"I don't know; they didn't tell me."

"But you know something."

"It's something to do with the last trick."

"The new one."

She nods. "After which I'm supposed to give you something."

I shoot her my stare. "Give it to me now."

"I mustn't."

"Why not?"

But Miss Porlock has turned away. She knows perfectly well I'm staring at her. You can tell by the indifferent way she tosses her curls and gazes at nothing in particular.

Uncle Asa swoops back onstage. "For our final act," he calls out, "we are proud to present an illusion never before attempted, one that's *extremely* dangerous!"

He scans the audience, then turns his head to the royal box. "Tonight, for the first time, we dare perform it in honor of His Excellency, the archduke, and his lovely consort."

His Excellency nods solemnly. The lovely consort raises one brow.

I'm used to knowing what happens next. I'm not used to being kept in the dark. I don't like it at all. Miss P. is muttering again.

The music swells. Mother appears in a pool of light.

In flowing silks and with a white silk scarf around

her shoulders, she stands perfectly still at the front of the stage, which has been built out into the audience. Behind her is a panel of black glass.

The crowd hushes.

The scarf begins to ripple, although there is no breeze. Then the little floating lights appear, swarms of them. She lifts her chin and stares into the distance.

I lean forward.

Slowly, the tiny lights orbit Mother. Soon I notice there are fewer lights than before. And less of my mother! Parts of her dress, her arms, her hair, are just not there!

More lights disappear. More of my mother disappears.

She's dissolving in front of my eyes!

The audience begins to realize what is happening. Ladies peer through opera glasses. The archduke, in his box across the way, gets abruptly to his feet.

The last points of light blink out. The place where Mother stood is bare. That's not quite true. Her white scarf flutters down and drapes itself on the edge of the stage.

An ovation erupts and continues for minutes. Asa returns, bows deeply, blows a kiss to the cheering audience, then turns, his arm extended toward the wing, welcoming his sister onstage.

His arm remains extended, but she does not appear. "Marina," he calls above the tumult of the crowd, "come out! They want to see you!"

No Marina.

Miss Porlock and I glance at each other.

"What's happening?" I mouth.

No answer. She gazes at the stage with a strange intensity.

The applause dies down, but Mother continues not to appear. "I think my beautiful assistant is playing with us," Asa says with a laugh. "Come now, Marina dear. Your audience awaits!"

No Marina Thummel. Murmurs ripple through the crowd. The archduke speaks to one of his aides, who nods and hurries off.

Abruptly, the stage curtain jerks closed. A moment later, I hear a loud crash, like glass breaking. I'm out of my seat and running, with portly Miss Porlock huffing along behind. I know my brain isn't working right, because the same crazy words keep churning inside me: *Mother! My mother has evaporated!*

Chapter Two

Backstage is in chaos. Asa flashes by, barking orders to the stagehand, Benny's father, who stands there fingering the strap of his overalls.

"Speak, man! You were right there, working the curtain!" When the fellow doesn't answer, Asa strikes him across the shoulders with his silver-tipped cane.

He hits him again just as two officers arrive. They look at each other, uncertain whether to intervene. A moment later, they're joined by one of the archduke's guards—a more decisive type—who grabs the cane out of my uncle's hand. No one pays attention to me. I hurry past, heading for the dressing rooms.

Nothing out of the ordinary there—Mother's feathered dressing gown and gold-heeled slippers flung about as usual, her creams and lotions strewn on the vanity, a white rose on the side table.

I can feel her, very close, very present. And very absent.

At first, I don't notice the envelope, then recognize the careless handwriting:

For Asa—Private

I hold the envelope up. Turn it over. There's her seal, the black wax impressed with a rose within a circle. The scent of perfume leaks from within.

I *have* to see it, but her seal warns me off. Not my business.

But couldn't I just peek? Break the seal? Who would notice, with everything else going on? This is a terrible time to be honest.

Just give it to Uncle Asa, like a good girl.

Returning up front, I'm shocked to find one of the officers holding up Marina's silk scarf and questioning my uncle. The conversation is not friendly.

The scarf, I see now, has small splotches of red near the bottom edge. Impossible not to think of blood.

"It's no secret," the officer says, his eyebrows slanting inward to make room for his frown, "that you and your sister have been less than"—he searches for the word—"*amicable,* if you take my point."

"What *is* your point?" Asa draws himself up to his haughtiest height. His mustache twitches.

I think I'll wait on giving him the letter.

Heading off on my own again, I check the storage room, even the boiler room in the basement. The watchman by the stage door is no help. Swears he's seen nobody.

Pain catches at my side, as if I've been running. *Stop breathing so fast!* Standing in the semi-dark, I remember the sound of breaking glass after the curtain was yanked shut. Yes! I run to the front of the stage, and there it is: a tall mirror on a flexible stand. The glass lies in shards, like black ice, over the floor. I bend and pick up one of the pieces.

"Ow!"

Stupid me! I suck on my finger.

Maybe that's how blood got on the scarf?

Here's something odd. The glass is black. I hold it before my face, but it doesn't reflect. What good is a mirror that doesn't reflect?

I want to tell Uncle Asa about this, and the letter. I find him by himself, his face furrowed, and slip the envelope into his hand. "I found this in her dressing room," I whisper. He stares at the letter, then moves away to open it. Turns it over and back again and reads it another time. Then folds the paper and tucks it in his pocket.

An officer approaches, then a second. More questions. Uncle Asa turns brusquely away, but the first officer grabs his arm. Asa wrenches free.

"I'll have to ask you to come with us," says the officer.

"I don't have to answer your idiotic questions!"

There is almost a scuffle. Finally, Asa stops resisting, and the officers push him down the hall.

I feel bad. *Hey, that's my uncle!*

No one notices the piece of paper on the floor. I seize it, unfold it, read it twice, then again, trying to tease some sense out of it:

Dear Brother—
   Your lies have kept me here too long. Now that I've wormed the truth out of you, let's see how well you do without me. I'll be watching.
   I offer a parting gift, since I know how much you want what I have. Here's how to get it. Inhale the scent of a pure black rose. But it must be purest black—blackness itself. Do this, and your search will be over.

It's signed with her usual slapdash, almost illegible *Marina.*

I'm confused. *You want what I have?* What does she have that he wants?

Oh.

But if it's so easy to get—just the scent of a rose—wouldn't Uncle Asa already be brimming with Marina's magic?

Wait! What's happening? As I stare, the last letters of Mother's signature fade away. Then the rest of her

13

name. Her note is erasing itself backward! Now only "Dear Brother" remains.

I know Mother can do tricks like this. I've seen her. But she's not here to do them!

I need to talk to Asa. I run to the back and catch up with the officers out on the street. They're opening a carriage door and setting the step beneath it. One of them holds my uncle firmly by the arm.

"Uncle Asa!" I call out.

He turns and sees me. "Go away!"

The officer gives him a shove and he steps in. The door bangs shut, and the carriage lurches ahead, leaving me alone in the street.

Chapter Three

"That reminds me," murmurs someone behind me. I whirl around. It's Miss Porlock, holding a small envelope. Her eyes are strangely excited. "I forgot to give you this. Your mother—"

I snatch it from her hand and tear it open. The familiar rose scent suffuses the blue notepaper. The message is brief:

The Arethusa. 11 o'clock. Tell no one.

I glance at Miss P.

Her eyes hold a question.

I walk away, reading the note over and over, but old Porlock stays with me.

"What *is* it? You must tell me! I care about her, too."

"What," I whisper, "is an *Arethusa*?"

"It's a ship. One of the ships down at the dock."

I hesitate, then hand her the note. Miss Porlock scans it greedily. Her eyes harden.

"She wants you to go there," she hisses (her version of a whisper). "It seems she's finally noticed your existence."

"What do you mean?"

"She wants you to meet her and go away with her!"

"Do you think so?" *Not possible*, I'm thinking.

"What else could it mean?"

I feel myself trembling. I am not a trembler. Ask anybody.

I don't want to finish the thought, but it finishes itself. Mother and Asa have been feuding. Even the public knows about it. Several times, she called him a fake, and of course, she was right. He may say she's his "beautiful assistant," but it's Mother who gives whatever real magic the performances have. He's the showman, but she's the draw.

Is this her way of ruining his career?

But why would she want *me* to come with her? Cisley the pest.

That stitch in my side is starting again. *Breathe!*

"Miss Porlock, if anyone asks you where I've gone—"

"You can't go alone."

"Of course I can."

"You're twelve years old."

"I'm almost thirteen. What does that have to do with it?"

"I'm going with you. You don't even have money for a carriage."

"Do *you*?"

"Enough."

I consider that. "Okay, but we've got to go right now. The boat might be sailing!"

I wish I had something warmer to wear. A fog is sweeping in and with it a chill that makes people stay inside. Not a carriage in sight. The cobblestones glisten. At last, an empty cab clatters by, and we climb in.

It's a relief to let Miss Porlock take charge. She knows everything, even how much the man should be tipped. Of course, she's an old person. Forty, at least. I watch her face as the streetlamps flit by and am surprised by an expression I haven't seen before—a suppressed smile, as if she has a secret.

Traffic thickens as we approach the port. "We'll get out here," Miss Porlock calls to the driver. Even a block away, the ship, bathed in light, looks enormous. A horn blast goes right through me, and I start running.

There are two gangways. Dockworkers struggling with steamer trunks jam the one for freight. The passengers' gangway is crowded with warmly dressed travelers with parcels, hatboxes, canes, even a birdcage or two. It's colder than before, a strong breeze blowing in from the Adriatic.

17

A porter lugging a heavy duffle bumps against my shoulder and scowls, but I scarcely notice.

"Mother!" I call out uselessly.

Miss Porlock, meanwhile, has located an official with a clipboard and inquires if a Miss Thummel is among the passengers.

"Thum, Thum, Thum," he murmurs, running a finger down the list. "Hey," he shouts suddenly, "wait, you!" and dashes off to collar a boy sneaking up the gangway, ducking among suitcases. "Where's your ticket, young man?"

He lifts the child by the nape of his ragged coat. "As I thought!"

"Wait!" Miss Porlock calls after him; but he's carrying his prisoner off and disappears in the crowd.

Most passengers are aboard now.

Mother, where are you?

The note said . . .

A bell clangs, my heart right along with it. Several large men prepare to haul in the gangway, while on the deck the ship's band strikes up a patriotic anthem, full of thumping oompahs and blatting trumpets. I look around desperately. Except for well-wishers waving handkerchiefs and porters wheeling empty carts, few of us are left on the dock.

I bite my lip, then make a sudden dash for the boat, ignoring Porlock's shout behind me.

My hands waving, I call out, "Wait! One more passenger!"

The gangway is just lifting away as I jump onto it and

sprint toward the deck. A worker shouts at me, but I'm already past him, flinging myself into the crowd of passengers.

I blur past a swatch of blue, which registers as a uniform with a loud voice: *"Just a minute, you!"*

In the thick of the crowd, several women attempt to move aside, but there's no place to step.

A glimpse of the uniform—just behind me now, a hand reaching . . .

I drop to my hands and knees, and scramble wildly through a jungle of legs. A woman squeals, a man loses his balance, falls backward.

I hear the band and scuttle toward it.

"Stop that girl!"

A flash of gold up ahead—the bend of a tuba. A hand rakes my back but doesn't get a grip before I'm among the polished shoes and instrument cases of the players.

A trumpet, seeking a high note, veers wildly higher as the musician dodges away, bumping into the drummer, whose snare drum tilts over, taking the cymbal with it.

I ignore the crash and scurry on. Behind me, cries of alarm. Ahead is a door.

Just get to the door.

I yank it open and run headfirst into a man's large belly. It's another officer, a bigger one. He grabs my squirming body and doesn't let go.

"I'm meeting my mother!" I scream.

The other uniform arrives, breathing hard.

"She says her mother's here," says the big one, struggling to hold me.

"*Mama!*" I scream. "*Mama!*"

"Calm down, kid," he says. "What's your mother's name?"

I'm so crazy that for a few seconds, believe it or not, I can't think of her name. "Thummel!" I finally burst out, like I'm spitting a peach pit. "Marina Thummel! She's my mother!"

"Your mother, so you said."

The band resumes, making talk almost impossible, although a small crowd has gathered around us. Everyone's staring at me, among them a serious-faced man in middle age, arms folded across his chest.

Go away, if you're not going to help.

The uniforms consult among themselves. Soon an official appears with a passenger list under his arm. He nibbles a frayed mustache and flips through the pages. "No one by that name."

"As I thought!" cries the first uniform.

It takes two of them to wrestle me off the ship and onto the splintery dock, where I sit whimpering.

Miss Porlock comes over to help me up.

A tremendous horn blast makes my heart jump. Engines churn, and soon, almost imperceptibly, the great ship slides from the pier. At the railing, passengers wave wildly. Kisses are blown, tears shed.

I keep scanning the passengers by the railing. No sign of Mother. There's that man again, the one who was staring at me before. A serious face, weathered. Am I supposed to know him?

The boat gains open water. The music grows tinny. Miss Porlock's heavy arm drapes itself around my shoulder. "We might as well go back," she says quietly.

I don't move.

"Cisley?"

I'm not listening.

The ship's lights grow dimmer until they're swallowed in darkness.

Chapter Four

"Mother," I murmur. "Mothermothermother."

I've been doing that a lot lately. Pretty soon, if I'm not careful, I'll be muttering like Miss Porlock.

It was winter when we left Trieste. Now it's spring, but you wouldn't know it. I wrap my jacket tightly around me and squint into the light. I still can't believe Mother's gone. Was she even *on* the boat? Her name wasn't on the passenger list. Did she change her name so no one would find her?

Since our return, Uncle Asa has been making inquiries, even hired an investigator to follow up on clues, the few that were found. The ship, he learned, was headed down the coast of Italy to Majorca, off the coast of Spain. What would Mother want to do there?

And where does that leave me?

It leaves me standing here on a seawall at dawn with my pet lobster, watching the horizon. Different sea, different country, same me. No mother, no father. Never had a father. I used to ask about him when I was young, but never got an answer. Everybody has a father, but for some reason mine was a secret.

And now Mother.

People wonder why I come here each morning at first light to stare out over the Firth of Before. I'm not crazy. It's not as though I expect to see Mother sail into view. I stopped hoping for that long ago, when we returned home to Ravensbirk.

Returned in disgrace. Nothing was ever proved against my uncle, but nobody wants to hire a man suspected of murdering his sister. It seemed a good time for Asa to rethink his career. He doesn't use the word "retirement," but that's what it feels like.

I give a tug on the golden leash. Elwyn sometimes gets too close to the edge of the wall. "Don't you, Elwyn?"

He waves a feeler at me.

A lobster of few words.

People think I'm odd in my choice of pets. Hard to explain. Cats make me sneeze, dogs slobber. When I came across Elwyn in a tidal pool, he climbed daintily onto a rock, signaled me with his feelers, and made a smart-aleck remark about my hair. (My hair does get kind of wild out here.) I didn't mind. People think *I'm* a smart aleck, too.

Admittedly, Elwyn comes with problems. On our

walks, I have to carry around a bucket of water and set him in it every few minutes. Even Miss Porlock, in her wobbly voice, has asked what I can be *thinking*. Elwyn is a handsome animal, as lobsters go, especially now with the early sunlight glancing off his shell, but I didn't pick him for his looks. I picked him because he's a good listener.

Who else can I confide in? Uncle Asa? I don't think he even likes me. After Mother disappeared, he had enough sense of duty to take care of me—or at least hire people to take care of me. I asked him if we were going to stay here in Ravensbirk very long, and if so, shouldn't I go to school? He seemed amazed that I'd consider such a thing.

"Let me understand." (Stroking the point of his beard.) "You want to spend your days among commoners? Sons of fishmongers? Daughters of chimney sweeps?"

I just looked at him. I'm very good at my stare. "You know, Uncle, I can't understand why people have the idea you're a snob."

What do you do with a person like that? How do you tell him that you'd just like to talk once in a while to someone who's not three times your age? I nodded at his thuggish servant Janko, who is never far away and almost never speaks. "And Janko is your idea of brilliant company?"

Janko's brow lowered. That's quite a brow he has, but not much behind it.

Asa's smile was thin. "You sound like your mother."

"I wish I was more like her."

"You're on your way. Already you have the tongue of an adder."

Lovely man, my Uncle Asa.

That was yesterday. Better to be alone out here with Elwyn. I give a tug on the leash. Spun gold. Nothing too good for my little friend. "Come on, Elwyn. Don't be such a slowpoke."

He crawls reluctantly.

"With ten legs," I tell him, "you'd think you could keep up!"

He gives me one of his looks.

"I know. It's time for a dunk in your bucket, right?"

I do the honors. Let him paddle around awhile before we push on.

We arrive at the big rock where I like to sit. Nearby, the fishing boats bob in their slips. Beyond that lies the town, still wound in mist. And over the far hill, past the Gypsy encampment, the top of the old glass factory and the roofs of warehouses.

Up here, high above it all, I could hold the whole town in my hands, and half the sea. This is where the world is most magical. Not pretty, or picturesque, although tourists like to call it that, but literally magical, like an electric charge. Anything can happen at first light.

Oh no! Someone's been here.

Looking closer: a little wooden box. How dare they come here? This is *my* place!

I run my hand over the wood. Rosewood? Smooth

as a kiss, with a nicely carved cricket on the lid and leaf designs around the sides. I lift the lid. Empty.

Somebody will be sorry to lose this.

Elwyn and I sit watching the fishing boats get ready to set out. It's a fine show, and I'm getting to know the characters by sight. By smell, too. Miss Porlock tells me I smell things others don't. The distant wisp of smoke, for instance, from that old guy's pipe. Cherry-flavored tobacco, I think. Every morning, he walks his little white dog—as fat as himself—along the beach. (I can smell the dog, too, unfortunately.)

A young fisherman is pulling nets from the wall and loading them on a skiff. And way far off, that solitary fellow I so often see—white pants, blousy blue shirt— just now setting up his easel and opening his paint case. Don't you love the smell of oil paint?

Commoners.

So why do I feel this sadness? This . . . envy?

I leave the little box on the rock and pick up Elwyn, returning him to his bucket and covering it with a tea towel. "Let's go, old pal. Time to head home."

The path grows sharply steeper as we approach the castle. Maybe you've read about the place in the tour books: the Crystal Castle. Overlooking the harbor, it perches on an outcropping of rock—or just *above* the rock—because as you approach, you'd swear the huge thing is floating ten feet off the ground!

That's Uncle Asa's mirror work for you.

I admit it's impressive, like a spiral of ice, flinging

colors through its hundreds of prisms. There's no fisherman's cottage down in the town that doesn't get a flash of color at some time during a sunny day.

Tourists line up for the chance to pay ten shillings and take a tour of the place. "Got to feed the beast," Uncle Asa says. The beast is the public. The beast also feeds him. The money keeps servants paid and food on the table.

Even before he built this monstrosity, Asa Thummel was the most important citizen in Ravensbirk. His fame put this little seaside town on the map. He could have been mayor.

Instead, he just owns the mayor.

When you pass through the castle's outer gates, you face a labyrinth set with tall rows of hedges, many of them trained into the shapes of animals. The patterns change. If you find the right path one day, you have to find a different one the next.

Since I'm in on the trick, I walk right through and sweep past the footman into the entrance hall. Too early for the tours, thank goodness. The visitors' desk is empty.

To me, the castle is more mirage than building. Asa's illusions give a sense of endlessness to the mirrored hallways and the star-crusted dome of the ceiling.

Feed the beast.

"Miss Thummel?"

"Yes, Mr. Strunk?"

The house steward, as short as his name, raises an eyebrow slightly, as he always does at the sight of

Elwyn's bucket. Those fluffy, flyaway eyebrows make him look angelic or devilish, depending on his mood. He's somewhere in between today. "Will you be wanting breakfast?"

"Yes, please."

"For two?" The eyebrow again.

"Just lizard bits for Elwyn."

"Very good, miss."

"Oh, Strunk, have you seen my uncle this morning?"

"He's taken his breakfast in the laboratory."

"He must have gone up early."

"He's been there all night."

I hesitate. "What's he doing there, do you know?"

Strunk hesitates back. "Doing, miss?"

Why is it so hard to get a straight answer to a simple question? "Never mind," I tell him. "We'll be upstairs whenever you have breakfast."

"Very good, miss."

I mount the curving staircase. Not his fault. Strunk has been forbidden to discuss his master's activities with his master's nosy niece.

Approaching my rooms, I hear a soft thumping within. Anna is moving books so she can dust behind them. She curtsies as I come in.

I curtsy back. It's a joke between us. She's been ordered to curtsy to her "betters," and I've told her not to. (Who am I to be curtsied to?) But Anna must follow rules or be fired; so now we curtsy to each other—and laugh.

I don't have friendships with other chambermaids,

but Anna is young and quick, with big Gypsy eyes. And she doesn't question me. Ever since I let her have my tortoiseshell hair clip, I can do no wrong. If I want a lobster for a pet, that's fine with her.

She's using the clip today. It gives a nice swerve to her cascade of black hair.

"I like what you've done," I tell her.

"Is nutting," she says, touching the side of her head.

I lug Elwyn's bucket to the bathroom. My thoughts turn to Uncle Asa.

"Elwyn," I murmur, crouching beside him, "we're going to find out what he does up there."

Truth is, I'm worried about my uncle. He's been spending more and more time in the laboratory, built on the castle's roof, between turrets. It's one of several areas of the Crystal Castle I'm not allowed to explore. Sometimes he doesn't appear all day, coming down at night, irritable and haggard, for a silent supper. It makes a long meal for me at the far end of the table. I got permission for Miss Porlock to join us, and that helps some, not that my tutor's a great conversationalist. We talk quietly, laugh seldom, aware of the silence at the other end.

Maybe it sounds like I hate my uncle, but I don't. It's been hard on him these last months. He's used to dazzled crowds and amazed applause, and here he is in exile, stuck with little old unamazed me.

I fill the dragon-footed bathtub with tepid water and add a scatter of seaweed powder to make it cozy.

"In you go."

"Thanks, Cis," says Elwyn—or seems to say. It's hard to tell, sometimes, with submerged crustaceans.

I gaze at him. "Have a nice swim."

Courtly as ever, Elwyn bends two feelers in my direction, his version of a bow.

Chapter Five

It's chilly out here, but worth it to watch the change from gray to blue, the upward bulge of light beneath the world, and finally that first direct shot of sunlight across the water.

Elwyn is not impressed, but he seldom is. At least he doesn't mind me babbling about it as we make our extra-slow way along the seawall toward our sitting place. When we arrive, my heart does a little flip. *They've been here again!* The rosewood box is where I found it before, and now, beside it, is a little wooden horse!

I turn it around in my hand. A pretty piece of work, but who could be so forgetful—*twice*?

No one in sight.

"Do you see anyone, Elwyn?"

I'm half convinced it was left for me. "Is anybody here?"

Listening, listening.

A crazy idea darts through my brain: *Mother left it! It's a secret message from my mother!*

"Hello?"

Of course not. If she isn't dead, she's on the other side of the world. I stopped expecting to see her months ago.

So why do I keep expecting to see her?

Below, where the shoreline curves like a protective arm, the town begins to stir. First to appear are dockworkers and fishermen. At the far end of town, there's movement among the tattered caravans of the Gypsies. Closer by, I detect the smell of frying sausage. Finally, the first of the Ravensbirk shopkeepers steps outside, broom in hand, to sweep the walk.

No one looks like a carver of horses.

I squint into the sunlight. Black glass, black glass. The mind's a funny thing. Here I am by the beautiful Firth of Before, and I can't stop thinking about a broken mirror on the floor of an empty stage.

But I've seen that glass somewhere else. At least its frame—dark wood, tall, with scrolled corners. I close my eyes and watch blobs of orange light float across my vision.

Mother's bedroom! (My eyes spring open.) Right here in Ravensbirk. Didn't she have a mirror like that in her bedroom? I was in that bedroom once. . . .

"Come on, Elwyn. Let's go!"

He looks at me questioningly. After all, we just got here.

"Come on. I mean it!"

Mother's suite of rooms has always been off-limits, except for those rare times when she'd invite me in for what she called girl talk. And strangely, I'm never quite sure how to get there, even though we're on the same level, what Asa calls the Mezzanine. Between her rooms and mine, he constructed a Mirror Maze, which tourists (for an extra fee) are led through three times a day.

He has the corridors reconfigured every night, and the sliding walls re-angled. Today, I discover, the hallway leading to Mother's wing has been hydraulically raised at one end, so that any attempt to reach her quarters will send you sliding back where you began.

All this is a demonstration of my uncle's great magical powers, I suppose.

While I stand there thinking, I detect light footsteps, a moan of metal wheels, and, yes, a hint of wisteria mixed with perspiration. Anna!

She comes in sight wheeling a laundry cart, then stops beside me and pushes back her hair.

She curtsies. "Hello, Miss Tummel."

I curtsy back. That always brings a smile. I especially like her calling me Miss Tummel. "Anna, I need your help. I have to get to my mother's rooms."

Her smile fades.

"Really. I need to get there. But as you see . . ." I indicate the glassy hill behind me.

She shakes her head.

"What is it?"

"I cannot lose my job."

"Why would you lose your job?"

"Mr. Strunk, he tell me."

"He tell you—he told you what?"

She nods at the tilted hallway. "Do not say people how it works."

"But I'm not people."

"You *are* people. He says your name."

Now *there's* a depressing thought.

"Okay. Just get me past this one thing. I'll find my way after that."

She looks doubtful.

"Anna." I look at her seriously. "It's important."

She directs her frown at the laundry cart, then nods, walks past me, and approaches the wall. She grasps the edge of one of the mirrored panels. It is on a hinge, and behind it are several switches. As I peer over her shoulder, she pulls the top one down. There's a loud groan from underneath us as the floor subsides to flatness.

"Wonderful!" I take her hands in mine. "Thank you."

She looks down.

I start off. Where, I have no clear idea, but I've gone on these expeditions before. I've even made maps and floor plans to help me remember where I've been, but with each new configuration of walls and floors, it's a different castle every day.

Ah! Mother's door! Heavy, oaken, dark, with a distinctive golden latch. I sniff the air. Odd. Why the smell of straw? The whiff of ammonia? I pull the door open. A broom closet!

I can almost hear Asa chuckling.

I continue on, the corridor darkening as I circle an aquarium stocked with glowing fish, then enter the dazzling brilliance of the Mirror Maze. Suddenly, a dozen Cisleys stare back at me, one of them fat and two feet tall, another with a mustache of butterflies, as if I needed to look worse than I already do.

I've never liked the way I look. Still mostly flat-chested, with a tangle of brown hair I can't do anything with, and freckles! *Freckles!*

I won't even mention the bony nose. You could use it for a sundial.

Nice eyes, though. "You have such nice eyes, Cisley." That's what grown-ups tell me when they can't think of anything to say.

Sea green.

The one feature I inherited from Mother. Green eyes. They look better on her. Everything does. What chance do I have next to "the most beautiful woman in Europe"?

You can bet *she* never had freckles.

I push on through the maze, narrowly avoiding myself, stepping on my face beneath my feet. And an added confusion: why am I smelling *flowers*? Amid all this glass? I follow it, and the scent grows stronger. At last, flushed and out of breath, I fight free of the maze, make my way down a familiar-looking corridor, and find myself before a thick wooden door. Same golden latch as before.

Broom closet?

From underneath, the smell of roses is unmistakable. Roses and cologne.

I try the handle.

Locked. Of course! Everything is locked around here.

The maids have to get in to clean, don't they? Maybe Anna has a key. I should have asked. But I remember now. As house steward, Strunk keeps all the keys himself, locking and unlocking each room as needed. It's not really his job, of course. It's not even the butler's. It's the housekeeper's. But in this secretive place, everything is controlled from the top.

I grab the handle, pull on it, rattle the door, then rattle it harder.

No use.

I turn back the way I came, fumbling my way through the maze, around the aquarium, past all the twists and turns of Uncle Asa's twisted brain, back to my rooms.

Chapter Six

Next morning, eager to get to the seawall again, I duck Elwyn in his pail and hurry down, ignoring his complaints. As I reach my sitting place, I get a jolt. The rosewood box is still there, and the wooden horse beside it; but something new has been added: a comical-looking, big-eyed turtle, in mahogany, its head poking out of its shell as if searching for something.

I approach the little figurine as if it were an explosive. Suddenly I'm *sure* I'm not alone. "Okay, who's there?" I call out, loud enough for even the dockworkers to hear me, if they wanted to. *"Come out!"*

Nothing. The only thing coming out is Elwyn, who has crawled from his bucket.

I peer into the shadows of boulders and scrub trees

beside the wall. A faint smell reaches me—a hint of sweat?—before a side wind snatches it away.

"I *mean* it!"

Slowly, from behind a rock ten yards away, a head appears.

Not my mother. Not nearly my mother. Why did I think it would be?

Next, the shoulders appear. A *boy*, for God's sake! A beggar kid, by the look of him, in his worn work pants.

We stare at each other in silence. Not that it's silent out here. Thirty feet of wind separate us. I hold out the turtle. "Is this yours?"

He shakes his head.

"Whose, then?"

"Yours."

The voice is calm. Calmer than mine. I wish the wind would quit whipping my hair around my face. "Why?"

He steps out from behind the rock. Bare feet. "I thought you'd like it."

I move closer. Twenty feet of wind between us. Elwyn starts holding back, and I give his leash a tug.

"Why would you care what I like?"

He shrugs. Shrugs!

I give another tug on Elwyn's leash. "Do you have a name?"

"Cole Havens."

"Coal? Like coal from the ground?"

He laughs. It's a good laugh, and it allows me to laugh, just a bit. Elwyn's the only sourpuss here.

"No, of course not," he says. "It's a perfectly regular name."

"Well, I never heard of it."

"Well," he says, "who ever heard of *Cisley*?"

So he's a smart aleck.

Ten feet of wind swirl between us. Not even the wind can disguise how much he needs a bath. But, okay, he's definitely a nice-looking person. All cheekbones and eyes. Dirty blond hair completely out of control.

He cocks his head to the side. "Do you really talk to that lobster?"

"What?"

"People say you talk to the lobster."

"Why wouldn't I?"

"Because . . ." He seems to be deciding how to put it. "Lobsters can't talk?"

"They *don't* talk. Not usually."

We're five feet apart now, and I can see his expression change. I know what he's thinking: *So she really is crazy.*

Who cares what he thinks?

"They also say you're a snob," he says. "Are you a snob?"

"Oh yes."

The answer seems to please him. "Me too."

I take in his shabby appearance. "What do you have to be snobbish about?"

"Phonies. I can't stand phonies. Are you a phony?"

This Cole person is getting annoying.

"You tell me," I answer.

That makes him laugh out loud.

"What's so funny?"

He just shakes his head.

"So you can't stand phonies," I say. "What else can't you stand?"

"Mice."

"Mice?"

"Can't get rid of them. Our house is down by the wharf. Mice and rats all the time."

"Lovely. Get a cat."

"We're going to."

I don't know why this conversation has turned into a contest. "Were they expensive?" I say to change the subject.

"What?"

I hold out the turtle. "I hope you didn't spend too much." The way he looks, any amount would be too much.

"I didn't spend anything. I made them."

I hope my mouth didn't drop open. "You *made* them?"

Cole's about to answer, but instead he lets out a loud yelp of pain. "Ow! *Shit!*"

Now there's a word you don't hear in the castle.

The lobster, seeing the boy's bare feet, has clamped a powerful claw on to his ankle, drawing blood.

"Elwyn!" I drop to my knees and pry the claw open. It's not easy. "Stop that, you horrible creature!" I plunk him into his pail.

The boy has dropped to the ground, gripping his foot. "I don't think your friend likes me," he says through gritted teeth. His hands are covered in blood.

I can't help myself. "You're not doing it right."

"What?"

"You're not doing it right. Here. Let me." I kneel. I take his foot and wrap both hands tightly around it.

Cole looks determined not to cry out again, but it's a near thing.

Here I am on my knees, holding a strange boy's foot. Not what I thought I'd be doing this morning.

As always happens, the wounded place starts getting warmer. Very warm.

"Hey! What's going on?" he says, alarmed.

Maybe I shouldn't be doing this. I make a note to wash my hands.

After another few seconds, I release the foot and examine it. The bleeding has stopped, and the gash is definitely smaller than before. The foot's just as dirty, however. I take hold of it again and bend over it with closed eyes.

"Hey," he says. "My foot feels hot!"

"It's supposed to." Doesn't he know how to fix a cut?

"Ow! Stop!"

"Don't be such a baby." Finally, I let go. As expected, there's no trace of blood; in fact, no sign he's ever been cut. "It should be all right now."

He scrambles to his feet and steps back, fear in his eyes. "How did you *do* that?"

"What do you mean? What do *you* do when you cut yourself?"

"Put a bandage on it, of course."

"A bandage. Why would you do that?"

He looks confused. "Maybe because I don't know magic?"

"Magic!" I have to laugh. "I don't think so."

"No, really."

"My uncle's the magician."

"And you're not?"

I look up at him. "I'm just a girl."

"Just a girl," he murmurs. There's something extra in his look that makes me uncomfortable. I get to my feet to break his gaze, but that's worse, because now we're eye to eye, two feet apart.

"Well," I say, picking up Elwyn's pail. "If you're okay now, I'll be going."

He looks down at his foot, turning it from side to side. He still thinks I've done some amazing thing. I think his *carving* is amazing. I slip the wooden figures in my sweater pockets.

"Thanks for these," I say. But I can see he's thinking of something else.

If he's not going to say anything, I'm going to leave.

Partway along the seawall, just before it curves, I look back. The boy stands where I left him. The wind makes a racket between us.

"The turtle's very funny," I call to him.

"He's supposed to be," he calls back.

We stand there, taking each other's measure for a few more seconds. Strangely enough, I don't feel awkward. The distance helps. If we could always talk at twenty paces, I'd be fine.

"Well," I say finally.

He nods.

I turn the corner, and he's gone.

Chapter Seven

Some days, I just feel bad. I think about Mother. I ignore Miss Porlock. I hurt Strunk's feelings. I don't know what I'm doing here.

I just called Strunk a horrible little man. I knew it wasn't true when I said it. He's not horrible. He's a very nice little man. Well, he can be. He refused to give me the key to Mother's rooms because he *had* to refuse. Uncle Asa would fire him.

It's Asa I have trouble with.

I feel around in my sweater pocket for the little turtle Cole carved, with its comical expression. It has become my good-luck charm.

That's another thing. What's Cole up to? He wasn't there yesterday or this morning. No more carvings left for me on the seawall.

Did he decide he doesn't like me? Was it all a dare? Did he go back to his friends and tell them how he finally met the Mystery Girl of Ravensbirk, and she wasn't so much when you saw her close-up?

Oh, and she really does talk to lobsters.

From where I'm sitting, halfway up the glass staircase, I can see the whole atrium below. Saw Asa go out a few minutes ago to talk with the chief mechanic. His magic depends a lot on mechanics and groundskeepers and optical experts. Something's always going wrong. Today, it's the outdoor labyrinth. A movable metal plate beneath one of the hedgerows has seized up—rust in the gears or something—making it impossible to change the configuration. The whole section has to be dug up.

A flutter of voices makes me turn. A dozen tourists troop down the staircase, led by a chirpy young woman from the visitors' desk. Normally, I'd flee to the kitchen and take refuge with Mrs. Quay, but I'm too depressed to move. I just scooch to the side and let them pass.

"Oh, here's Miss Thummel!" pipes the tour guide, flipping her hair. "She's Marina Thummel's daughter. Hi, Cisley!"

I manage a wan smile. Everyone stares at me as they pass, some whispering. This is an unexpected bonus for their admission fee: the daughter of the magical Marina!

One young girl, maybe eight years old, approaches me. "What's it like living in a glass castle?"

The others pause to listen.

It's a question I get all the time, but for her it's the first time in the history of the world.

"It's . . . magical!"

She beams, nods vigorously, looks around at her friends. "I wish I could live here!"

"What fun that would be!" I answer. *As long as you don't have an uncle like Asa standing over you.*

The group continues on and files out the back way, since the labyrinth is closed for repairs. The girl turns and waves to me. I wave back.

Uncle Asa is still outside. He usually spends his days in his rooftop laboratory. Guess he's not doing that today. Guess I won't be getting into Mother's rooms, either. But I've *got* to see if the mirror is there.

I plod upstairs. Time to feed Elwyn. Then there's Latin with Miss Porlock. Oh joy. Outside the door, I pause. I don't want to go in.

What's the choice?

"Cisley, is that you?" Miss Porlock's shaky voice sings out from my sitting room.

"Hi, Miss P." I poke my nose around the corner. There she is, a dumpling of a woman in the chair by the window, sunlight glancing off the bulge in her forehead. A porcelain teapot and the usual plate of ginger cookies are beside her. She bakes them herself and thinks I like them.

Latin can be fun, like figuring out a puzzle or learning how to talk to Elwyn; but today I'm too jumpy. "Say, would you mind if we skipped our lesson this time? I don't feel very well."

"You're never well when we discuss the ablative case. Have a ginger cookie," she says. "It will buck you up."

I sigh and slump into a chair. There's no escaping the ablative. I bite a brittle cookie and open my book.

An hour later and three pages into Cicero's second oration against Catiline, I'm free to go. First, I look in on Elwyn. My little friend seems content to crawl around in the bath. After a quick check of the water temperature—tepid, the way he likes it—I give him a wave and slip out.

To my left, a staircase spirals up to Asa's laboratory. To my right, past a confusion of corridors: Mother.

I could try. Maybe I can figure something out.

Starting in that direction, I see the corridor has been hydraulically raised again, but I know about the control panel. A quick click, and the floor groans and lowers. I continue on.

Around the first curve, I run straight into Anna. She looks wild, distracted.

"Hi, Anna."

She stares at me with big eyes, then seizes my wrist and drops something into my hand. She closes my fingers around it.

A key.

"What's this?"

She shakes her head. "I cannot help you more."

"Is this . . . ?"

"My brother Nicolae makes it. I am careful, but Mr. Strunk suspects."

"Anna." I don't know what to say. She risked her job for this. "Anna, thank you."

I'm not sure she heard me, because she's already down the hall, not looking back.

With the key tight in my fist, I hurry on. But the way has changed since yesterday. Mirrors are realigned. Partitions have been re-angled. Even the aquarium is not a reliable landmark. Today, it's a mirror, the fish within it mere reflections. Where are the actual fish?

Then comes the Mirror Maze, which tourists seem to love. It's a source of revenue for Uncle Asa, frustration for me—all those twisted Cisleys! After blundering into glass walls and ducking under mirrored arches, I pick up a scent of, yes, roses and follow it. Down one blind alley, it becomes quite noticeable. How can it be strong here, if there is no way to go? Then I find a narrow glass panel that swivels aside, allowing me to slip through. The scent is more definite now, and before long I find myself in front of Mother's door.

I slide the trembling key in the lock. It doesn't turn. Anna's brother is no locksmith. I wiggle it, then work it harder, to wear down the rough edges.

Open, you!

No good. Here, Anna took this big risk for me, even got her brother involved, all for nothing. I could cry.

I take out the key and examine it. Scratches and file marks, as if it's been attacked. Wounded by clumsiness.

Could I heal it? Could I warm it enough?

I enfold it tightly and sink down along the wall to a crouch. I clasp my joined fists to my chest and bow my head. Soon the key grows warm, then hot.

Unbearably hot!

Agh! Teeth clenched, I grasp it tighter.

I can't do this! It's like holding a live coal in my hands!

Not yet! Not yet!

When I can bear it no longer, I feel the key bend slightly.

Try it!

I shove the key in the lock, give it a second, then turn it hard.

Click!

With a sigh, the door swings open.

But my hand! The skin's begun to blister. Pain surges from my palm halfway up my arm. I stumble into the room and peer through the semi-darkness. *There!* A white rose above the fireplace. I grab the vase and dash cool water over my hands.

Better!

Barely.

I look around. I haven't been here in months, but the room looks just as it did when Mother, feeling lonely one night, called me in. It surprised me to learn that she could be lonely, too. She never lets such emotions show. She's either cool or amused, when she isn't furious.

That night, she looked sad, as if it was all too much effort to be, what? Perfect?

I'd never seen her without makeup. I liked her better without it and told her so. She gave a little what-do-you-know laugh. And I remember thinking, *Why can't we always be this way, just natural?* She told me a little trick to do with my hair. (My impossible hair!) And that made me brave enough to mention something I'd always wondered about: those little points of light she sent out over the audience during her magic shows.

She hesitated. "It's a secret." But then she threw me a sidelong look. "It has to do with elementals," she said in a low voice, as if the drapes would overhear. "The astral light's full of them."

"But how do you make them *do* things?"

"They warm up. I don't know how else to put it. They warm up if you concentrate in a certain way."

"Show me."

She shook her head. "That's what Asa's always saying. He'd love to know my secret. But he'll never get it out of me."

I looked down. There was suddenly a big sadness in me. Why did it have to be this way?

She caught my look. "Here. Hand me that bottle."

I brought her a slim blue bottle from the vanity.

She shut her eyes in concentration, and soon a dozen "elementals," as she called them, hovered in front of me. She uncorked the bottle, and several tiny lights slipped in. She recorked it and handed it to me. "In case you need a night-light," she said.

A present. My mother giving me a present! I couldn't

stop staring at it, the tiny lights circling and weaving in their little blue world. "Oh, thank you!"

She nodded. "That's fine. Now you'd better run along. It's time for me to get my beauty sleep."

I was being dismissed without so much as a hug. But with an amazing present. I've kept it on my night table ever since.

Now, all these months later, entering the outer chamber—what she calls her sitting room—I trail my hand along a silk table runner. She loved elegant things, like the bronze sculpture of a rearing horse on the mantel. Beside it stands the vase with the white rose. On the floor beneath lies a puddle—the water I spilled on my burning hand. I stare at the rose. This is the flower that was calling me through the maze. Calling, as if it had a voice. Mother's voice. Yet all I can feel is her absence.

Only once—on that special night—was I allowed into the innermost chamber. I enter it now, heart hushed. It's her vaulted bedroom, the ceiling lost in dimness, the whole room suffused with reddish light, like a cathedral. I realize I have never seen the room in daytime. The glow is from sunlight pulsing through the red draperies.

I fling open the drapes for better light, and the room comes blindingly into focus. I'm searching for signs of the full-length mirror that used to live in the corner. Had I imagined it?

Wait. The crisp daylight reveals four sharp dents in the carpet. Yes, that's where it stood! So she *did* take it with her to Trieste!

Next to the canopied bed hangs the full-length portrait of Mother in a satin gown. And there's her walk-in closet. Is the gown still there?

Don't open the door. You have no right.

I fetch an oil lamp from the vanity and step into the closet, finding myself faced with rank upon rank of dresses, gowns, furs, hatboxes, shoes. Battalions of shoes.

How far back, I wonder, *does the closet go?*

Holding the lamp carefully, I move along the narrow aisle, dresses brushing against me on either side: "Shhhhhh," they say.

Is this a closet or a tunnel?

Halfway back, I notice a pure white evening gown, with a line of diamonds running down the side. Imagine wearing such a thing!

No one's looking.

As I drape the dazzling dress over my arm, I swear I see it wink at me. Back in Mother's bedroom, I hold it against me in front of the vanity mirror.

Mother's taller than I am, and fuller in places a tomboy like me can only dream about. I change out of my things and slip the gown over my head.

The sensation is indescribable, like a hundred caresses. I shrug the shoulders snug, give the sides a little tug, and again look in the mirror.

Not possible! It fits me *perfectly*, taken in where I'm smaller, tucked where I'm narrower. Even the length has been altered as though by invisible hands.

"Mother?" I whisper.

I sit down on the bed and stare at her portrait.

I remember looking at the picture that long-ago night, half thinking it was the painting of a goddess, a mischievous one, with just the slightest smile tweaking the corners of her mouth. She stands straight, her white neck elegantly long, one hand resting on a pedestal, the other holding a black rose.

In the shadows behind her—I hadn't noticed this before—there's a tall mirror on a stand, but turned away from us, perhaps reflecting the moon in the painting's background.

I stare at her face, at her eyes, at the black rose she holds so lightly in her hand.

Black rose, white rose.

Mother, who are *you?*

Chapter Eight

It's my birthday today. Well, well.

In celebration, Miss Porlock and I are out on the town, a great concession on Uncle Asa's part. Truth is, if it weren't for Miss P., there wouldn't be a celebration at all. Every year, she appears in my sitting room, holding a tart with a candle in it, and sings her little song. Then it's off on an excursion somewhere. One time, it was a carriage ride in the country, another time a picnic by the cliff. It's a chance for her to talk about important things—Romantic poetry, fabrics for dresses, and the princes I will someday marry.

I remember only one birthday that didn't have the Porlock touch. I must have been five or six. Mother threw an extravagant party, importing children I didn't know from the village, showering me with presents, and performing magic tricks. I got overexcited and came down with a fever that night.

And that was it, as far as Mother was concerned. I don't think it occurred to her that this was something that should happen again. It was a sort of motherly meteor shower.

But this year, says Miss P., I have an important birthday. I'm turning thirteen, and I deserve something special. A closed carriage takes us to Pendleton's, a dry-goods emporium in the better part of town, where my tutor makes an examination of all the fabrics in from London, asks my opinion, then disregards my advice. It is her chance to play the great lady, and I wouldn't deny her a minute of it.

She tells me to pick out anything I want, anything at all. The place is full of so many things that I'm sure I'll find something wonderful. Turns out they're wonderful if you're Miss Porlock's age. I finally find a charm bracelet I like, and she buys it for me.

Soon she's lost in reverie among the shawls, arranging one around her broad shoulders and making a coquettish turn before the mirror.

"What do you think?" she asks about a blue paisley.

"Perfect!"

"I don't know. I don't think it goes with my coloring."

Miss Porlock doesn't have coloring, unless you count gray. Still, it touches me to think Edna Porlock was once a girl hoping to be pretty.

From Pendleton's, it's to the pharmacy for Miss P.'s

eyedrops and anti-itch cream, then to the tea shop for a treat. My tutor sheds her cape but keeps on the shawl, the blue paisley one. She couldn't resist it and now can't be parted from it.

The scones here are actually good (well, compared to Miss P.'s ginger cookies), and I'm allowed—because it's my birthday and my companion is feeling so devil-may-care—a strawberry ice, topped with whipped cream.

The light outside the window begins to lower, and the passersby step a little faster. We all know about afternoon rain showers in this part of the world. I loll a Maraschino cherry in my mouth and look out.

A crash and a gasp make me whirl around. "Oh!" Miss Porlock cries. She's on her feet, holding the front of her dress, a wisp of steam rising from it. Even the new shawl has been spattered. A broken teacup lies on the floor.

The shop owner hurries over, and she and I do what we can. Soon all is well, or almost. Dear, clumsy Miss P. This is not the first or the fifth time she has broken things.

The worst thing to be broken is her mood. It takes me a while to get her smiling again, and I succeed only when I draw her out about fabrics. That sends her into a happy daydream, and before long I'm free to look out the window and have daydreams of my own.

Miss Porlock is going on about woolen tartans or something when I notice a commotion across the street. It's hard to see with the rain starting, but there's no mistaking two kids, a boy and girl, racing from a clock shop, the boy holding something under his coat while the girl, smaller, narrow-faced, struggles to keep up. A moment later, the storekeeper bursts from the shop and chases after them.

The children dart past my window, and for a split second I see the faces clearly.

Cole!

"My dear!" exclaims Porlock. "Are you all right? You don't look well."

I forget to remember to answer.

Cole? A *thief*?

I don't want to see him.

I want to see him.

Elwyn and I are on the seawall, watching the sun come up. Though it's late spring, the wind is almost cold.

"I told you not to trust him," says Elwyn quite distinctly.

"You told me nothing of the kind."

"Don't you remember? I clawed his foot."

"That I do remember."

"I could hardly have been clearer."

I look down at the lobster perched at the edge of the wall. "Why don't you like him?"

"Other than the fact that he's a thief?"

"You didn't know that then."

Raising one of his heavy claws for emphasis, he turns

to me. "What do you expect from a boy like that? Did you see how he was *dressed*?"

"I think you're as snobbish as my uncle."

"That would be difficult."

"Agreed."

Elwyn turns in his slow and delicate way to look over the harbor. "So, where is this boyfriend of yours? In prison?"

"Elwyn, stop it!"

We don't speak to each other for most of a minute, but his question has hit a nerve. Where is Cole? Is he ever going to show up again?

"Quit worrying about him," says Elwyn, picking up on my thought. "He can't help you."

"Can't help me what?"

"Find your mother, of course. Isn't that what you want?"

I'm almost too surprised to answer. "Of course that's what I want. Don't torture me with the impossible."

"Why impossible?"

"Elwyn, she disappeared five months ago, on another continent. I'm just a girl standing here, talking to a ridiculous lobster."

"You're a Thummel. That means something."

"But what can I do?"

"Think. Who else was there when your mother disappeared?"

"Uncle Asa."

"And what do you suppose he's concocting up there in his hissing laboratory?"

"I have no idea."

"Don't you think you ought to have an idea? Think like a Thummel. Stop being a weak girl mooning over a ragamuffin."

"I've never heard you talk this way."

"It's about time you did. Now get me back in that bucket. I'm parched."

We head home in silence. Approaching the gate, I see the labyrinth is still closed off. A great pile of dirt stands by the hole where mechanics are working on the underground metal plates. I go around to the side entrance.

Once in, I hear my uncle's distant shout.

"Good morning, Miss Thummel," says Mr. Strunk, a model of composure.

I glance down the corridor. "What's he mad at today?"

"New dining chairs have arrived. Master Thummel is not happy with them."

"*Strunk!*" Like a magic trick, Uncle Asa appears to step out of a column halfway down the hall. His black shoes click on the marble.

"Sir?"

Asa pulls up beside us, gives me a glance, then turns to his steward. "Strunk, I hate a spool-turned leg!"

"Sir?" Mr. Strunk glances nervously at his own calf.

"They disgust me. Stacks of billiard balls, that's what they look like."

Strunk looks lost.

"I think, Mr. Strunk," I murmur, "my uncle is talking about chairs."

"Of *course* I'm talking about chairs. Now, what's his name, the crippled fellow who fixed the Chinese side table last year?"

The steward's face brightens. "You mean Havens, the cabinetmaker."

"The very one. Get him here."

Asa finally notices the covered pail under my arm. "What have you got there? Not that filthy reptile, I hope."

"Elwyn is not a reptile, and he's cleaner than we are!"

Asa's eyes narrow.

"I bathe him twelve times a day. He even sleeps in the bathtub!"

"In the bathtub! Worse than I thought. Get rid of that disgusting creature right now!"

"Uncle Asa!"

"Or send him down to the cook. At least he can serve some purpose."

I pale at the thought.

"I'm serious. I can't have you making a laughingstock of us."

I start to object, but he holds up a silencing hand. "I know what people are saying. It's not Asa Thummel the magician. Not anymore. It's old Thummel, uncle of that peculiar girl who goes about with a filthy whatever-it-is. I won't have it!"

"He's my friend."

"Your friend."

"I know that sounds odd to you."

"It sounds absurd to me."

There's no way to make him understand. "You're not really angry at *me*," I say finally.

"Oh, I am."

"You're angry about the chairs."

"That, too."

"And you're mad about the chairs because you're mad about the labyrinth."

I can see this isn't getting me anywhere. In fact, he's smoldering. "And?" he says, his eyes flashing.

But here I hesitate.

"And why am I angry about the labyrinth?"

No. This is a minefield I mustn't cross.

"Say it!"

I look down. "Nothing."

He's moving from angry to furious. "You think I'm mad about the labyrinth because I have to rely on incompetent mechanics, is that it?"

I say nothing.

"And I have to rely on incompetent mechanics because—why? Why do I have to rely on incompetent mechanics?"

"Because . . ." He knows and I know, but it's bad to say it. "Because you don't have magic."

I see his fist clench and unclench. The moment passes. He mutters through his teeth: "Get rid of the lobster. *Today!*"

He turns on his shiny leather heels and clicks off down the corridor.

Chapter Nine

"You know," says Elwyn as I lift him from the bathtub and set him, dripping, on the tiles. "It may be just as well."

"What do you mean? It's terrible!"

"Did you see the way the cook was looking at me today, when we went through the pantry? It's only a matter of time before she drops me in a pot of boiling water."

"Don't say that!"

"Especially considering the way your uncle feels."

"Who are you talking to?" Miss Porlock's voice reaches me from the other room. She comes to the door. "Oh."

"Elwyn says I need to let him go."

"Elwyn? You still think that creature can talk?"

"Of course."

"Don't you remember your biology? Lobsters have no voice box. They barely have a brain."

I turn to Elwyn. "I know you don't like to speak when others are around, but say something. She won't hurt you."

"What should I say?" he says clearly.

"Anything, but speak up! She can help us."

"I doubt that very much."

"If someone hears you speak, they won't cook you!"

"Oh, that would make me even more of a delicacy. Delicious *and* loquacious!"

"Low what?"

"Look it up."

I turn to Miss Porlock. "You heard that, surely."

She looks at me with pitying eyes.

"Elwyn, say something else."

"Why? Only you can hear me. Don't you know that?"

"What do you mean?"

"We talk mind to mind."

"Mind to—?" I turn to my tutor. "You really don't hear anything he's saying?"

"Oh my dear," she says.

Elwyn lifts a feeler. "The tide should be high soon. Maybe we should go."

A glance at Miss Porlock tells me there's no help to be found. I fill Elwyn's bucket, set him in it, and hurry out.

* * *

The path to the seawall is a shambles of loose rocks and dirt, and partway down I slip and nearly fall, whacking the bucket on the ground.

"Hey!" Elwyn calls from inside.

"Sorry."

"My shell isn't made of iron."

I reach my lookout spot and watch the waves dash against the rocks below. Cole isn't anywhere to be seen, but I no longer expect him. He's probably out filching goods from shopkeepers or laughing with his friends about Thummel's crazy niece.

And who's that girl he was with, running from the shop? Accomplice? Girlfriend?

I climb over the edge of the wall and work my way down to the water, balancing Elwyn's pail in one hand while I search for handholds with the other. It's loud down here, waves curling and crashing. To my sensitive nose, the smell of seaweed and dead horseshoe crabs is startling.

Slowly, Elwyn emerges from his bucket. He's free of the leash but still wears his spun-gold collar. He seems to like it, so I leave it on him to remember me by.

For long seconds, we stare at the water. "Where will you go?" I say.

"The firth's a big place."

"Will I ever see you again?"

He is silent.

"Elwyn, will I *see* you again?"

"You'll hear from me."

Somehow, that's not reassuring. "Why are you being so mysterious?"

"You'll hear from me. One way or another. Probably another." He steps delicately into the water. A wavelet sweeps over him, bearding him with foam. "Don't forget what I told you," he says.

"About what?"

"About that mad scientist you call your uncle. Pay attention. He's up to something."

"And how would *you* know what he's up to?"

"You mean," he says, turning his beady eyes on me, "how would I, a mere crustacean, a pair of ragged claws—"

"That's not what I mean at all."

Another wavelet, foamier than the last, briefly covers him.

"Never underestimate a crustacean, my dear," he says, sputtering slightly. "And now, if you don't mind, I've got a tide to catch."

"Won't you miss me?"

It takes him several seconds and another wavelet before he answers. "I will miss you very much, Cisley Thummel."

With that, he steps farther out and is immediately submerged. For another few seconds, I can see the glimmer of his golden collar. Then he really is gone.

We're in the heat of the day now, and the boats have left for the fishing grounds. The painter, having done what he could, folds his easel and trudges along the beach. He lifts his hat to wipe his forehead with his arm, and I see his face.

Something about him: the tan, deeply lined forehead, the serious eyes. Haven't I seen him before?

Not here. Where?

Why does it disturb me?

I lean back against the seawall and watch.

I *know* I've seen him before.

Chapter Ten

I'm out in the hall, listening. Not a sound.

The tightly spiraled staircase lies to the right—to Asa's rooftop laboratory. What would he do if he caught me up there?

But this morning, he's outside. I saw him with Strunk, inspecting the labyrinth.

I wish I had Mother's courage. But even a coward can put her foot on the first step.

Why haven't I ever been allowed up there? I can understand why he doesn't want outsiders seeing how he invents the effects for his magic show, but I'm family; I know his tricks; I've seen the smoke in all his mirrors.

I take the second step. After that, the others are easier. As I round the first curve, a slight breeze reaches me from above. The next curve brings me a faint scent of flowers.

Heavy thudding above me. Coming nearer. But Uncle Asa's outside!

I snatch off my shoes and pad back down the stairs, trying not to make a sound. The footsteps are louder and closer. I make it to the bottom just as Janko, my uncle's assistant, clumps into view.

"What you do here, jong lady?" His voice is heavy and slow, as if words aren't natural to him.

I take too long to answer. He grabs my arm, hard enough to leave a mark. "You were going up dere, no?"

My heart's blasting away.

He shoves me so roughly I bang against the wall. I clutch my shoes to my chest, an image of my mother flashing through my brain. How disappointed she would be. *You're a Thummel. Act like one!*

"Guess I took a wrong turn," I murmur.

Janko purses his lips, deciding whether or not to kill me. "Go," he grunts.

I slip past him down the corridor.

Still shaking, I stick my hand in my pocket and touch my wooden turtle for luck. "In times of stress," my mother once told me, "always keep your bowler on." That didn't make much sense to a girl who would never think of wearing a man's hat, but it means something now. Always carry on. Don't give in. In my case, at this moment, it means going down to the pantry and getting a snack.

The cook—portly Mrs. Quay—and Jenny the pantry maid both like me, the cook, I think, because her own children have all grown up and moved away, and Jenny because she doesn't have any. I sit on a stool by the work counter and swivel back and forth while they gossip and feed me candied walnuts.

The subject of gossip today is Uncle Asa's latest tantrum about dining chairs. The chairs still aren't right.

"He can be a terror, your uncle," says Mrs. Quay.

I nod, wondering, *Are we ever angry about what we think we are?*

I *have* to find out what he's doing up there.

Stuffing an almond cookie in my pocket, I thank the ladies and hurry to the atrium. Through the front gate, I can see Uncle Asa and Janko talking. I'll never have a better chance than now.

I run to the second floor, then patter up the spiral staircase to the roof. In a moment, I reach the relief of open air, amid flashing scimitars of red, blue, and yellow light that ricochet between the crystal walls and glass-paved patio. It's like being inside the sun, without the heat, or on top of a glacier, without the cold. Overhead flies a canopy, green and flapping in the wind, while just beyond, nestled between glittering turrets, stands the laboratory: a squat structure with glass walls to let the sunlight in.

Uncle Asa's secret.

No surprise that the door is locked, but I can see through the glass. On a long worktable, pots of flowers stand like patients in a hospital ward, many of them attached to machines, tubes, cables. And all of them roses: dark red, dark brown, dark purple, in various stages of growth or decay.

The words from Mother's letter swirl in my head: *Inhale the scent of a pure black rose. But it must be purest black.*

Of course. But why does he care so much? Surely his own tricks are spectacular enough. He's practically a genius at them.

They're not enough. Of course they're not enough. I never realized it so clearly before. It's real magic he craves.

Something on the worktable catches my eye, next to the line of test tubes: a jagged piece of glass. Hard to see, but from where I stand, it looks black.

Black rose.

Black glass.

Black . . . magic?

All within the dance and dazzle of refracted light.

I am now desperate to get inside. I examine the door. If I broke one small pane, I might be able to reach through and undo the lock. *Yes, but think about it. When Asa gets back, he'll see what I've done. Then what will I say?*

Cross that bridge later. I glance around, searching for something, anything. The patio is bare except for a hedge in a long flower box and the canopy overhead. Hanging from it is a metal rod that you turn to retract the canvas.

That might work. I reach up and try to detach it. It's surprisingly heavy and fights me, but I twist it free.

Hefting the pole like a battering ram, I aim for the pane beside the door. Easy now. Slow down.

I lunge and strike the glass with a loud crack. I've hit a corner of the pane. A web of lines radiates outward, but the glass is intact.

I hoist the metal pole again and steady myself. Careful. This should do it.

I lunge forward, but immediately I'm yanked *backward*! I spin around. *Uncle Asa!* His eyes burn into mine!

Neither of us says anything, each of us holding on to the pole with all our strength. He rips the thing from my hands, flings it aside with a clatter, then slaps my face. I hit the floor hard.

"How dare you!" he roars.

I groan. The fall hurt much more than the slap, my cheek gashed on the edge of the metal flower box, and my hip throbbing.

"Look at me!" he shouts.

Not possible. My cheek is bleeding, starting to swell up, partly closing one eye. A fuzzy image of Asa's face swerves over me. His momentary fury has changed to something else. A frown scrolls his forehead. "You're bleeding."

I must look pretty bad for him to care. I lick the corner of my mouth and taste blood.

"How can you be so clumsy?"

I don't reply.

"We'd better do something about this. Janko!" he calls out. *"Janko!"*

"Never mind," I manage.

"No. You're going to need a bandage. And I don't want to hear you whining about this. You brought it on yourself."

"Never mind!" The sharpness of my tone surprises me. I cup my hands over my puffy cheek, my eyes closed in concentration.

"Look," he says, his anger lessening, "you need to put something on that."

"Shh!"

His anger may be lowering, but mine is rising. I can hardly remember the fearful girl I was before his slap woke me up.

He starts to say something, but I cut him off. "Will you be *quiet*?"

After a few seconds, I feel the heat building on the left side of my face. It grows warmer, then actually hot. Uncle Asa is speaking, but I can't listen, can't break my concentration. I feel the swelling subside, the pain leak away. Give it another few seconds, to make sure. When I lower my hands, I can see Uncle Asa clearly. His look has changed to astonishment.

"What did you *do*?"

"What do you mean?"

"Just now. The bruise is gone! The bleeding—"

"How about my lip?"

He continues to stare.

"The lip," I say impatiently. "Has it stopped?"

He nods blankly. "It's . . ." He seems to lose the thread. "It's perfect."

I nod. Getting to my feet is painful. I'll heal my hip later, when I'm back in my room. Hard to explain how I feel. I'm not at all afraid of this man. What I am is furious. He's never hit me before, as bratty as I've been. I can guarantee he'll never do it again.

"Look," I say through my teeth, "I can't talk to you now. But I've got some questions, and I'll want answers."

He's still looking at my face. "Yes, yes," he murmurs.

As I limp away, he speaks to my back: "I'll have some questions for you, too, young lady."

Chapter Eleven

No thanks. I don't plan to face my uncle over the dinner table, even with Miss Porlock between us. I reach for the tapestried bellpull and call for the chambermaid, a pleasant, mostly silent woman in her fifties, and ask to have supper brought up.

The truth is, I'm famished. I get hungry when I'm angry. He hit me! He hit me hard! I'm all right now, after giving my hip the special hands-on treatment.

The vaulted window looks out over the waters of the firth. Somewhere out there, my little friend Elwyn is scuttling about making a new life for himself—or making a meal for someone else. I should have taken off that golden collar. Unwanted attention.

Thinking about him, I almost don't hear the soft knock on my door. I hurry over to let the chambermaid in. But it is not the chambermaid. It's Uncle Asa, carrying a tray!

"May I come in?"

May he come in. Mind if I slap your face first?

I step aside.

He glides past, enveloping me in the scent of hair pomade, and sets the tray on the side table. Showman to the end, he whisks the silver dome from my dinner plate, releasing a glory of mingled smells: duckling, buttered beans with almond slivers, and cheese-infused potatoes.

"May I join you?"

"What if I say no?"

He takes a seat opposite me. "Too late."

I notice he has brought no food for himself, only a glass of ghastly liquid he calls Calvados. It's his favorite drink. Smells like kerosene.

He sips, frowns at his glass, and sets it down. "You said you had some questions. I thought it best if we dealt with them in private."

"All right," I say. "Here's one. What were you doing with that broken glass?"

"What broken glass?"

"The glass from the black mirror. I saw it on your worktable."

His brows lift, to give his eyes more room to see me. "I'm impressed." He swirls the drink in his glass and sets it down without having any.

I wait.

"I suppose that explains why you were trying to smash your way into my laboratory."

I wait. I'm really good at waiting.

"What was I doing with the glass? I was analyzing it. It came from a mirror, as you say, but it doesn't reflect."

"I know that."

"You seem to know a great deal."

I don't answer.

"It's very old," he continues. "I remember seeing it in our mother's room when Marina and I were children."

That stops me. "You mean it's been in the family—"

"For generations, probably. Nobody would tell me what it was for."

"What *is* it for?"

"Wish I knew." This time, he does take a drink. The mixture of alcohol and hair pomade takes my appetite clean away. "I've tested it every way I can think of."

"No luck?"

He shakes his head.

"No black rose, either, I assume."

His look of surprise borders on fear. "Wh-what—" He actually stammers. "What do you know about black roses?"

"That letter from Mother? I read it. Actually, I watched it disappear from the page."

"She's always been proud of that trick."

"So," I say again, "no black rose yet?"

He gives a hollow laugh. I don't care for the smell of

his breath. "There's just one problem, a small detail your mother failed to mention." His eyes grow hard. *"There is no such thing as a black rose!"* He pounds the table. Several beans fall off my plate.

"I don't understand. There are pink roses, yellow—"

"There is no black rose because black is not a *color*!"

"I'm confused."

"It is the *absence* of color. Don't you understand? It sucks all colors into itself. We are talking now about pure black. There are plenty of *dark* roses, but they—"

"They're not magical."

"Think about it. A perfectly black rose would be *invisible*!"

"Mother must have known that."

"Of *course* she knew it. She took no end of pleasure in mocking me." He pauses. "There is something about it, isn't there? A black rose. The color of mystery, if anything is. The noncolor, I should say."

I don't think I've seen him like this before. He's often quiet, but it's the quiet of calculation. This is different. He stares into his glass. "It's everything we can't see. The dark side of life. Death. Passion."

"Magic?"

He darts me a look.

"So, you believe her, then? You think that if you can manage to create a black rose—"

"I wouldn't be the first to try. People have been obsessed with it for centuries. A few have come up with very dark roses. But when you look closely, they're really dark purple. Or dark maroon." He pauses. His pause lasts a long time. "Let me know when it's my turn to ask a question."

I brace myself. "Go ahead."

"I'd like to do more tests."

"You need my permission?"

"I think so. You see, I'd like to do them on *you*."

My shoulders tighten. "I think you tested me quite enough this afternoon."

"This afternoon, I didn't know what you were."

"What does that mean?"

"I didn't think you had possibilities." He puts his hands together, prayer-wise, and rests his chin on them. "I didn't think you were interesting."

"What makes me interesting now?"

"You have something I don't."

I make a face.

"*Magic*," he says. "It runs in the family. Correction. It runs in the female side of the family."

"And you think—?"

"Don't interrupt. I'm making a confession, in case you didn't notice. I don't make them very often." Uncle Asa drains his glass. "I can't tell you how strange it was," he says, "growing up with a mother who could pluck eggs out of the air and then make omelets out of them. Marina had her own abilities. Different abilities. She could make print disappear from a book. Or appear. She could make a torn shirt mend itself." He gives a little hum of a laugh. "She could make half of Europe fall in love with her. That's a sort of magic, too."

He pauses. "Apparently not all magical people can do the same things. I wouldn't know. All I knew was I couldn't do any of them." He looks off into the distance. "A simple accident," he murmurs.

"What accident?"

He shoots me a look, realizing, probably, that he's been talking to me as if I were an actual person, not just some bratty creature he's been saddled with. "It's odd," he says. "Through the simple accident of being born a male, I'm left outside. Locked out."

I nod, taking this in.

"While my sister, my selfish, undeserving sister, is handed the keys to the kingdom."

"Keys?"

"*Magic!* I'm talking about *magic!*" He looks at me hard, and his eyes are wounds.

Not the kind I can heal.

"And now along comes little Miss Cisley, the next female in the line. She has no idea what she's about, and yet she heals people by touch!"

"Well, there's more to it than just touching, Uncle Asa. You have to—"

"Spare me."

I stare down at my dinner. It hardly registers that the objects are food. "I still don't see—"

"Come now, Cisley. You aren't stupid."

"Thank you."

We sit for some seconds in silence.

"So you want to test me?"

"I want to see what you can do. The extent of your abilities."

"Why? Why do you care?"

"Aren't you interested in your abilities?"

"Of course I am!"

"But you never tested them yourself?"

"I didn't know I *had* them. I thought everybody healed things that way."

"You really have been isolated, haven't you?"

"You noticed."

He tilts his head, assessing me. "What's come over you? You never used to be like this."

"Like what?"

"Talking back. Challenging everything I say."

"You're right. I was afraid of you. Silly me."

"And you're not now. What happened?"

"This afternoon happened."

He sighs. "About that. I didn't actually intend—"

"Let's not go into it, if you don't mind."

We fall silent. He pulls gently on the end of his nose, his lids half closed.

I'm assessing him, too. Those crafty eyes. "You're not interested in me, Uncle Asa," I say at last. "You just want to see if you can use me."

He smiles slightly, just a quiver. "I *knew* you weren't stupid."

Chapter Twelve

Tonight's visit from Uncle Asa upset me badly. His sudden interest after months of indifference—years, really—turned out to be selfish after all. What did I expect?

I stare at my blue night-light, with its bright elementals floating eerily about. Usually, it helps me get to sleep. At least helps me smile. Not this time.

A bright rectangle of moonlight lies across the floor, like a letter slipped through the window; but it's blank, a letter from no one.

I swing out of bed and pad to the bathroom. That makes me think of Elwyn and his bathtub swims. Where is Elwyn when I need him?

And Mother?

And that mysterious being known as a father?

How often I've fantasized about meeting him, by

chance, on a street in a foreign city. Fantasized about what he'd look like, what he'd wear. He'd be handsome, of course. And hurt in some way that kept him from coming back to us, although he wanted to. Longed to.

No one here will tell me anything about him. It's like he never existed. Did he do something shameful? Is he in prison? Did he die in a shipwreck?

I stand in front of the bathroom mirror and tell my reflection it's okay to be lonely. It's okay to feel this icicle lodged in my chest. It's just part of me. Maybe it always has been, even when Mother was here. Here and not here.

Without my loneliness, would Cisley be Cisley?

Without his woundedness, would Asa be Asa?

I go and push the window open. Beneath the full moon, the town is tightly tucked, the firth a coverlet drawn up to its chin. Butcher, baker, candlestick maker, all asleep. All with families to dream about. And here I am—in a castle, no less—without mother, father, or friends. I've been *kept* from having friends. I thought Cole might be one, but it looks like he's got all the friends he can use. Even a girlfriend!

And how much of a friend can Miss Porlock be, kind as she is? Tonight, ten minutes after Uncle Asa left with my untouched tray, Miss P. timidly knocked, avid to know everything.

"He wants you to *work* with him?" Porlock shook her graying curls. "That doesn't sound like Asa."

"Surprised me, too."

83

"Are you going to do it?"

A shrug isn't much of a response, I know.

"Cisley?"

"I don't know. Sure. Why not?"

"He forbids you to go anywhere *near* the laboratory, and now—"

"I know."

"I don't know what to say."

I turned to her with a weak smile. "You could say good luck."

"Oh, I do say that. I do."

Dear old Miss P.

Sometime before dawn I must have fallen asleep, because when I open my eyes I'm on the window seat, my body stiff, and the maid is knocking with my breakfast.

Food and a bath help shake me awake. I'm ready to explore. Out in the corridor, I turn in the direction of Mother's rooms. The floor is level today, but before I go far, I'm confronted with that damnable Mirror Maze, reconfigured and more confusing than ever. Many of the glass panels reflect me in some grotesque form; but several reflect people I know. There, just to the right, stands Mr. Strunk, one hand in his pocket, jingling his keys as he inspects the wiring behind a panel.

"Mr. Strunk!" I call out, heading for him through prisms of glass. I almost bloody my nose bumping into a mirror that is not a mirror at all but a clear window.

By the time I reach the place where Strunk was, he's nowhere to be seen. He was never there to begin with.

What does Asa need real magic for when he can do this?

I feel my way forward—or is it backward?—through this glowing ice cave of reflections. Rounding an invisible corner, I see up ahead a reflection I never would have expected: *Cole Havens!*

How did Asa know about Cole? How did he manage to capture his image in the glass? And a greater question: how did he animate that image to make Cole appear to look up at me and smile?

"Well," says the image of Cole.

I'm speechless—not usual for me. I feel my way forward, catching a strong whiff of sawdust, sweat, and . . . *Cole!*

I break into an astonished smile that's a moment away from tears. I touch his arm. "Is it you?"

He laughs in a way not even Asa could counterfeit. "I'm not sure. I'll have to reflect on that."

My mouth must be open, but no words come out.

"Actually," he says, "I'm lost."

It takes a few seconds to remember I'm angry at him. "What are you doing here?"

"I was looking for you."

Don't you try that boyish smile on me!

"I was easy enough to find," I answer in my hard voice. "I've been down at the wall every morning. As you *know*."

He looks at me as though I've said something odd.

"How did you get in?" I continue.

"Getting in was easy. The hard part is getting out."

"Have you come here to steal from us?"

Ha! For that, he doesn't have an answer.

"What," he manages to say, "put that idea in your head?"

"Simple enough question." I level my special stare. "You're a known thief. You sneak in here—"

"Where did you get the idea I was a thief?"

"Don't deny it. I saw you running out of that shop last week. You had a big bundle under your coat, and the owner—"

"You saw *that*?"

I cross my arms. A small army of cross-armed Cisleys surrounds the boy, all of them glaring.

He looks down with a puzzled smile. "You thought I'd stolen, what? A clock?"

"What else? You were running out of a clock maker's shop."

"Yes, I was. But with a cat."

"A *what*?"

"I got some memorable scratches that day."

"Wait. You were running."

"Ever notice how cats feel about rain? I was trying to get him home."

I don't believe him. I half believe him. I want a reason to hate him for not showing up on the seawall, morning after morning.

"Why was the owner chasing you?"

"I didn't know he was until the next day. He'd forgotten to tell me something about the cat."

I wait, arms still drill-sergeant crossed.

"He wanted to warn us not to feed him milk. Best mouser in Ravensbirk, but he can't digest milk. Unfortunately, we found out too late."

An answer for everything.

"We?"

"Me and Gwen."

"She's the girl—"

"She's my little sister."

Try not to look surprised. "Of course."

I shelve my other questions and cut to the important one: "So," I say, "what are you doing here?"

"Helping out my dad. He's redoing some chairs for your uncle. My job is to carve birds and vines on the chair backs."

I reach out and flick a curl of sawdust off his shoulder. "And somehow you ended up on the second floor, tangling with mirrors."

"Serves me right. I was looking for you."

"Here I am."

"Still angry?"

Good question.

"While you're making up your mind," he says, "can you show me how to get out of this place?"

"I'm as lost as you are."

"That's ridiculous! You live here!"

"Please tell Uncle Asa that when you see him."

It strikes me as funny that I could get lost between my rooms and my mother's, and never be seen again. Then another thought, equally silly: *Gwen. Gwen's his sister!* A giggle escapes me.

Cole looks relieved to see it. "Any ideas?"

"Let me think."

Yes, Miss Magic Girl, think of something.

"Wait. What do you smell?" I say. "Besides yourself."

He looks around, sniffing. Shakes his head.

There's that other ability I have. Is it possible for a sense of smell to be . . . magical? "Let's go this way."

He follows close as we slip around glass walls, past hordes of reflections. "It's getting stronger," I say over my shoulder.

"What is?"

"Roses."

On we go until, stepping around a final trapezoidal pane of glass, we find ourselves in a corridor a few yards from Mother's door.

I slip my key in the lock. Hesitate. Cole's never been here before. Is it violating Mother's privacy? I feel her resistance, like Elwyn when he'd pull back on his leash.

The scent of roses is strong.

I look around at Cole. He nods.

I turn the key.

Chapter Thirteen

Silence enfolds us. We walk softly, letting our eyes adjust, making sense of the lumps of dimness in the sitting room. I draw a match from my pocket and light a table lamp, turning up the wick. A white rose glows in its crystal vase.

A different rose this time, taller than the other. Who changes them? Who waters them?

Not watching my step in the semi-dark, I bump into Cole. He catches me by the arm. I'm more aware than ever of his boyness, the room's darkness, our aloneness.

"Quite a place," he says softly.

"Yeah."

I wonder if there's some way to bump into him again. But I remember where I am. Mother's sanctuary. She'd *hate* knowing a stranger was here.

And do I trust him? Do I still think he's looking to

steal something? This would be the place. He meets my glance. "These aren't your rooms, are they?"

I shake my head. "Mother's."

"Where is she?"

He doesn't know! "Don't you read the papers?"

"I don't believe them."

"You really haven't heard anything?"

"The other kids talk about it. They say your uncle killed her. Did he?"

I have an unreasonable impulse to defend Uncle Asa—although just last night, I wanted to ask the same question myself.

"Not that I believe what they say," he adds quickly.

"No, you shouldn't."

We fall silent. The place seems to want silence.

"So you're here looking . . . ," he says.

"I don't know what I'm looking for."

He glances around the shadows. "You want me to help?"

I ignore the zing of excitement and scan his face: the clear forehead, full lips, alert blue eyes so often on the verge of amusement. But not now. He's serious now.

"I've searched the place pretty thoroughly already, but . . ." I need to make a quick decision: trust or mistrust. Mistrust. Trust. "Okay," I tell him. "You'd better sit down."

He takes the flowered ottoman. I take the chair opposite and tell him about my mother's disappearance, the mysterious black mirror, the note she left me, the ship that sailed without me. Cole's a good listener, it turns out, almost as good as a lobster.

"You must have been very close to her," he says.

I take a beat too long to answer. "Very," I say. "So. About the mirror. It was back there, in the bedroom."

"Can I see?"

I glance at the darkness beyond the bedroom door. No one goes in there without Mother's permission.

I lead the way, carrying a lamp before me. The flame turns the room's red-tinted air to burnt orange. A finger of sunlight pokes through an opening in the drapes and throws a bright diagonal across the wall. Across the painting.

"Who's that?"

"That would be my mother."

He looks at the painting longer than absolutely necessary. "Pretty woman."

"People have said that."

"Not sure I'd trust her."

My heart beats harder. "Why do you say that?"

"The eyes."

"What's wrong . . . ?" I stop myself. I look at the portrait, trying to see it the way Cole does. Okay, maybe there's something about the eyes. Half mischief, half steel. The artist really caught her.

"She has her own picture by her own bed?" he says.

"What's wrong with that?"

"I don't know. Nothing. It just seems a little . . ." He catches my look. "Nothing."

I pull the drapes aside, changing the subject by flooding the room with light. "Over here is where the mirror used to be."

He studies the indentations in the carpet. "Not much to go on. Let's see if there's anything else."

I remind myself that I've decided to trust him. Still, I hold back. Mother glares at me from the painting.

No need to tell him about the dress I tried on.

I settle myself at the vanity, before the three-paneled mirror, her domain. Everything's neatly arranged: combs, silver-backed brushes, a glass tray with little bottles of perfume. I pull out the top-left drawer. Nothing any lady of fashion wouldn't have.

"Do you really have time for this?" I ask, turning to Cole, hoping he doesn't. "Don't you need to get back to your dad?"

"Yes, but remember? I don't know how to get there."

"Right."

"Maybe he'll send a search party after me."

"They'd get lost." I go to Mother's dresser and open the top drawer, feeling beneath her carefully folded clothes. All I find are sweet-smelling sachets and a number of silk stockings, some still with the Paris labels.

Cole takes pillows from the divan. "It would help if we knew what we were looking for."

I close the drawer and move to the bookcase. Novels by that popular lady author who writes under a man's name. More novels. Also a number of thin books that turn out to be poetry. I move on.

I feel something hard in my pocket. Cole's turtle. "I like him," I say, pulling it out. "He cheers me up."

"That's what I was hoping."

"You were?"

"I thought you needed some cheering up."

"Was I that glum?"

"You were . . . serious."

I think a moment. "Wait. How long were you watching me?"

He doesn't answer.

"Cole?"

"Long enough to figure out you were different."

I give him my famous stare.

"Different. You know. More going on upstairs."

What does that mean? I step on the ottoman to reach a silver decanter on a shelf. There's something in the bottom of it. "Cole. Come here."

He climbs up next to me on the ottoman. In my open palm lies a gold ring.

"Hello," he says.

I hold it up and squint to see better. "Looks like an inscription."

I feel his breath on my cheek. I've never been this close to a boy before. I wobble a bit, and he steadies me with an arm around my shoulder.

"To M," he reads, "with love . . ."

"From P," I finish. "This is a wedding ring!"

"*M* would be Marina."

My breath lightens.

"But why," he continues, "would she hide it?"

I can't think with him so close. But there's another excitement as well: the letter *P. My father?* This is the first clue I've ever found. Paul? Philip? Peter? What else? Phineas?

A loud door slams behind me. *"Just what is going on here?"*

I practically fall off the ottoman. Uncle Asa stands by the entrance, stiff as a fireplace tool. Cole lowers his hand from my shoulder.

"I'll take that, if you don't mind." Asa reaches up and snatches the ring.

He turns a cold eye on me. "And the *key.*" He holds out an impatient hand.

I stare back, fighting panic.

The hand stays out.

With a sigh, I dig in my pocket and give him the key.

"Sorry, sir," says Cole. "I got lost in the maze, and Cisley—"

"I'm not speaking to you."

"Yes, sir."

"Anyway, you're not lost."

"I'm not?"

"No," says Asa, his voice dead cold. "You're *fired!*"

"No!" I cry without thinking.

Asa looks at me. "Actually," he says slowly, "yes."

He turns to Cole. "Now get out!"

PART TWO

Nobody Sings at the Castle

Chapter Fourteen

There are problems with having a keen sense of smell. Uncle Asa's laboratory, with its vials of chemicals, pots of dying flowers, cages of lizards, and bins of compost— it's making me a little sick. After days of tests, I can hardly take it.

Or is it him I can't take? He fired my only friend! I should never speak to him again, yet here I am cooperating. The main reason is to find some clue, something that could lead me to Mother.

Asa, of course, thinks I'm here because I'm just wild to learn about my special abilities. Well, all right, yes, I am. Of *course* I am, now that I know I have them. But I'm not so sure I want *him* to know about them.

Working up here hasn't been fun, and it's gotten less fun as days go on and I keep failing his experiments. He's angry that I can't hear whispers through brick walls. Or *see* through brick walls. Or see *around* walls.

"Here," he says, taking a mallet and smashing a glass vial, "put that together. No hands." I'm supposed to re-assemble it through mental effort alone.

Now, *there's* a power I'd like to have, especially around Miss Porlock. It would save her so much embarrassment—and so many teacups.

"Why can't you do this?" snaps Asa. "Marina could do it when she was five years old."

"You told me yourself. Different people have different abilities."

"Yes. You can smell at a distance." His voice is acid.

The tests go on.

I'm bad, it turns out, at regressing butterflies to their pupal stage. Worse at making plants sprout before my eyes. Worst of all at making red rose petals darken to black. Asa is really disappointed by that one. He made me take that test three times. Each time, I saw him gritting his teeth.

I'm starting to feel disappointed in myself. There are so many things I can't do. Things it never occurred to me to do.

Levitation?

"That would be lovely," I tell him. (My feet remain firmly on the ground.)

Controlling the weather?

"That would be really useful in this rainy town. But no."

Turn invisible?

"I could walk out the door. Does that count?"

Ultimately, all the experiments lead back to the rose. Half the books on the shelf are about cultivation, hybrids, horticulture. I'm just the fallback. If he doesn't succeed with the rose, he might be able to use me in his act. He's practically said as much.

I've told him I'm not interested. It's fine that he wants to restart his career, but it's not for me. Not with him.

Most people would be flattered by all this interest, and I admit I'm excited. If only Asa weren't the one doing the tests. Asa is interested in Asa. I'm interested in Mother—learning if she's alive, getting her back safe. Uncle Asa has hardly mentioned her; and that piece of black glass I saw on the worktable last week is nowhere to be seen.

It's been a long afternoon after a long week—test after test—but for now, in one of those rare moments, I'm here by myself. Uncle Asa has been called downstairs to attend to "a servant problem."

I wonder who's getting fired.

Wandering around the lab among vats and bins, I have the odd feeling I'm looking at a picture of my uncle's mind, but jumbled, like a scattered puzzle. If the pieces were fit together, what would they show?

A thought zings through my head. It's one I've had before but discounted. If he is not trying very hard to find out what happened to his sister, maybe it's because he already knows!

No, he couldn't. Not his own sister. Could he hate her that much?

Now I'm hurrying from one table to another, pulling out drawers, looking on sills and shelves. It's got to be here somewhere. I pull down a tall leather-bound book. Nothing behind it but dust balls.

He should empty his trash barrel. My nose wrinkles at the mingled smells of rotting flowers, dead lizards, and who knows what else. I look closer, and a wink of glass catches my eye. I reach in. My God, there it is! A piece of broken mirror, ten jagged inches of blackness. *He threw it out!*

Breath catches in my throat. Footsteps!

I slip the glass into my cloth shoulder bag.

"Well," Asa says, easing the door shut, "that was interesting."

A sound of ripping fabric—the glass is tearing through my bag! I lower the bag carefully to the floor.

"You sound cheery," I say.

He smiles, not nicely. "It always bucks me up to fire incompetent servants."

"Not Strunk, I hope."

"Oh no." He pulls on rubber gloves and searches around in a terrarium, pulling out a white mouse. "I'd be lost without Strunk." He looks at me, his mouth tightening. "Well. Are we ready for some more tests?"

I'd rather face the Latin ablative. "All right."

"Good. Heal this!" he says, and neatly slices off the mouse's tail.

"That's *horrible!*"

The creature writhes on the counter, blood dribbling from its stump.

"Well, heal it!"

"I don't like you."

"Just do it, before it dies."

I bend over the creature, hold its severed tail against its frantic body, and blink away a tear. *Concentrate!* My hands grow warm. The wriggling diminishes. Now my hands feel actually hot. The smell of blood is strong as I let go of the mouse. The tail is fused to the body—but the animal is dead.

Asa pushes me aside. "Clumsy child! You *cooked* him! Come now," he says, seeing me turn away, "this is no time for squeamishness."

The look I shoot him is poisonous. "I don't want to do this anymore."

"You can't be soft if you want to be a magician." With his left hand, he brushes the dead rodent into the rubbish bin. "What *is* it?" he says. "Why are you looking at me that way?"

"What way?"

"Never mind. We have time for one more experiment. Let's get to work."

"No thanks."

"I promise not to slice up any more rodents."

"Glad to hear it."

"This next one's interesting. It's all set up." He goes over to the apparatus he's built. It's meant to test my ability to "precipitate," as he puts it—to make writing appear on a blank page. "Shall we give it a try?"

I'm a little startled by the idea. Writing tricks are one of Mother's specialties, as I saw last winter in Trieste, when her letter to Asa unwrote itself before my eyes.

Is it possible I could do it, too? I'd love to find out. But I wouldn't want Asa to know about it. He knows too much about me already. "I do better when I'm fresh."

He sighs. None of today's experiments has worked. "All right, get out."

"Thank you."

"But I want you back at seven tomorrow morning. We've got a lot to do."

Very carefully I lift my bag, hitching it on my shoulder. The glass clinks. He looks at me curiously. I give him a weak smile.

Hugging the bag against my side, I ease out the door, shut it gently behind me, and head for the stairs.

Chapter Fifteen

It's not like me to pace about like this, but back in my rooms, I can't stay still. Each time I pass the table, I glance at the jagged glass I've laid there. A blotch of nothingness. A spill of black ink. An absence.

I stop to examine it for the tenth time. What do I think I can learn that Uncle Asa couldn't, with all his cleverness?

The glass, pitch-black, has a sinister look. Turning it on edge, I see that the backing is thick lead. Why so thick? Protecting against what? I wish Cole were here to help puzzle it out. He may be a "commoner," as Uncle Asa has reminded me several times since that awful day in Mother's room, but he's smart. Also, for some reason, he seems to like me. (Does that mean he's not so smart after all?)

I see Miss Porlock has left a pot of tea for me, and more out of duty than anything else, I pour a lukewarm cup, swirling it absentmindedly as I circle the table. The mirror belonged to my mother and to her mother before her. There's another mystery. What did they *use* it for?

I set my cup down on it and stare out the window. In the late afternoon sun, the firth is blinding, as bright as the mirror is dark. I toy with a tortoiseshell hair clip, turning it around in my hands as I watch the first fishing boats return to the harbor. Directly below me, someone is leaving the castle, a woman lugging a suitcase.

From this distance, it looks like Anna.

Anna!

Suddenly I realize what I'm holding: Anna's hair clip, the one I gave her. She returned it!

I run for the door, down the curving staircase, and out through the atrium, only to find the labyrinth still blocked off. Reversing myself, I race down the great hall and burst through the door to the kitchen. Mrs. Quay looks up from the turkey she's basting, but before she can speak, I'm out the back door.

At the crossroads, I finally catch up with Anna. Her big eyes widen as I stand before her, gulping for air.

We don't say a word.

Uncle Asa's "servant problem."

She sets down the suitcase.

Silently, I hold out the hair clip. No reaction. I take her wrist and place it in her hand and close her fingers around it. The same as her gesture, I realize, when she gave me the key. She looks at me steadily, but I can't read her expression. Slowly, she gathers her long hair and snaps the clip in it.

What am I supposed to say? I'm sorry? She can see that.

I pick up her suitcase, and together we start off. She glances at me sideways. After a few minutes, she takes over. We trade the suitcase back and forth along the dusty road that circles the town.

The Gypsy caravan lies on the outskirts—four canvas-covered wagons drawn in a semicircle. With the nearest wagon still twenty yards off, we stop to rest.

A distant wrinkle of sound—someone's guitar. People mill about; a woman in a blue head scarf tends a cauldron over flames. The distant reek of work clothes mingles with wood smoke, the tang of cabbage with the savor of baking bread.

A figure separates itself from the others and hurries toward us. A little boy. Anna doesn't wait for him to reach her, but runs and grabs him into her arms.

"Hanzi," she moans, finally giving way to tears.

The music stops. The woman in the blue head scarf takes Anna in her arms, but no one comes near me. How different they look from people I know. What would Strunk make of their wind-burned faces, some with mouth sores, their burning eyes, their brightly patterned but flimsy dresses, with a chilly night coming on?

Anna sets her hand on the head of the boy and speaks in a language I have never heard. Hanzi tries to lift the suitcase, but it's too much for him. He gives it a yank, and the catch breaks, spilling Anna's sad possessions on the ground. For a moment, no one moves. Then Anna falls to her knees, grabbing at things and throwing them back in. I don't really want to see her rolled-up dresses, boots wrapped in newspaper, books, underclothes, crucifix.

An older boy comes over and kneels to help her.

She pushes at him. "Nicolae, go away!" He ignores her, slaps the suitcase shut, and hefts it under one arm. He shoots me a look that scares me. No one is happy, and I remember what Anna once told me: *I cannot lose my job.*

She speaks briefly to her mother, then turns to me. "You eat with us?"

My surprise must show, because she adds, "She want to tank you."

"Thank me? I've been nothing but trouble."

Anna shakes her head. "You are not trouble. Mr. Tummel, he don't like us. The key Nicolae makes . . ." Another shake of the head. "Is just a reason he gives."

She's right. If it weren't the key, there'd be something else. These are the kind of people Uncle Asa has warned me about.

"I don't understand. You're such a good person, Anna."

"We are Roma. Gypsy. People don't like us for tousand year."

I look around at the unsmiling faces. Well, one of

them is smiling. Little Hanzi. He's holding on to Anna's leg and grinning up at her.

People, trying to exist.

"So you eat? Yes?" says Anna.

"I'd like to stay. I would. But . . ."

The woman in the head scarf holds a hunk of bread in her dirt-hardened hands. *Mamaliga?* she says. Her voice is harsh, her face creased leather, but her eyes are bright.

I look to Anna for help.

"Corn bread," she says. A small smile starts along her lips. "*Mamus* wants you to eat."

I nod to the woman. "Thank you." Yes, her hands are dirty, but the bread is warm, the smell good. I break off a corner. "Well," I say, "maybe I could stay just a little while."

Immediately, the atmosphere lightens. People talk, children tumble and run, chickens scuttle. A boy pulls out a guitar. Lots of minor chords. An older man pulls out a harmonica and joins him. Then the boy starts to sing. A strange tune, but I like it. There's a yearning in it that I recognize, although I don't understand a word.

Nobody sings at the castle.

Mamus calls out, and the clan convenes for dinner.

What a difference from my solemn meals in the castle's dining vault, with the crisp white linen and throne-like chairs. Here, we are outdoors, sitting on the ground, with a steaming pot in the center. There are a lot of questions directed at me; luckily, I have Anna to interpret.

How many shoes do I own? Did I ever eat that lobster? Can my uncle really turn children into mice?

Anna's mother ladles a steaming concoction into wooden bowls, which get passed around the circle. *"Sak te mas,"* she says in answer to my questioning look.

"Meat and cabbage," Anna explains.

I don't know when I've had such an appetite. A big loaf of *mamaliga* is passed around, hand to dirty hand, and each person breaks off a piece.

I whisper to Anna, "Don't people use plates and forks?"

She shrugs. "We have saying. Food taste better from your hands."

I try to imagine what Uncle Asa would think about that.

Anna's mother comes up and speaks in a low voice. Anna frowns, looks around.

"What is it?" I say.

"Nicolae is not here. I don't know where he goes."

I remember that Nicolae was the only one who wouldn't speak to me. "He doesn't like me."

Anna looks at me gravely. "Is not you. Is Mr. Tummel. He is not nice. Also . . ." She pauses. "Also your modder."

"My *mother*?"

Anna looks down. "I should not say."

"What about my mother?"

"She has magic. But the Roma, we have magic also. Tousand-year magic. She don't like it."

"She don't? Doesn't?"

"I do not say more."

"Anna."

She tilts her head. "She make tricks on us. One time, she change *Mamus*'s shoes. She make for same foot. We are not laughing."

I don't know what to say. I've seen some of the tricks she's played on Uncle Asa.

A dog barks. Anna stands up. Then I hear it, too—a rumble of wheels over the rutted road.

Now everyone is standing, watching a coach roll up and stammer to a stop. The door opens, and a familiar head pokes out.

"Cisley!"

If ever I didn't want to see Miss Porlock . . .

"Come, Cisley. Your uncle is worried about you."

"I'm having dinner," I call to her. "Come and meet my friends."

Miss P. isn't about to step out of the coach. "Cisley, come right now. You can have dinner at home."

It occurs to me that I could refuse. I look around at Anna and her family. They're looking away. I'm once again that girl from the castle.

I turn to Anna, but she glances down.

"Anna."

"You better go."

"I don't want to."

She looks at me directly. "Your uncle will be angry."

"I don't care."

"*At us.*"

I stare at her. Would my uncle really make *more* trouble for these people?

Of course he would.

I look over at Anna's mother, but her face is unreadable. "Thank you," I call to her. "The food is wonderful."

I turn and climb into the carriage. Different smells. Instead of fire and boiled cabbage, it's leather and face powder. We jerk into motion, and I sink back in my seat and say nothing all the way home.

Chapter Sixteen

I trudge up the glass staircase. No dinner for me, thanks. Outside my door, I stop, reluctant to go in, reluctant to go anywhere.

A bath will make me feel better.

I step in the room, and my heart lurches. There's someone—Uncle Asa!—lounging on the sofa, head tilted to see me from a new angle.

"The traveler returns," he says, smiling. "Did you enjoy slumming?"

It takes me a few seconds to answer. First, my heart needs to slow down. "Do you enjoy firing people?"

"When they disobey the rules, yes, I do."

Sudden anger burns in my chest. "She was just helping me find my way. In my own house! What do you have against the Gypsies anyway?"

"Nothing at all. I have nothing against my horse, either, or my dog."

His words knock the breath out of me. "You don't . . . ," I start. But I need to start again. "You don't see them as people?"

"People of a sort."

"People like you and me?"

"Like you and me? No, my dear."

"They are, though."

"Well, I'm sure we could have a lively discussion sometime over dinner. Right now I'm just glad you're home safe, without being robbed."

"They didn't rob me. They fed me."

"Ah." He gazes at the ceiling. "I can't imagine what delicacies they must have served."

"Stew and corn bread," I say through set teeth. "We sat on the ground. We ate from the same pot. Sang songs. Laughed. All sorts of things we don't do here."

An unexpected smile lights his face. "Well, well! That got a rise out of you. Good!"

"Something else gets a rise out of me. Why do you have all these obstacles to keep me away from Mother's rooms?"

"It's not about you. People expect surprises. A magician's house needs to be interesting."

"It's not interesting, Uncle Asa. Somebody should tell you this."

"Others might disagree."

"What others?"

He waves his fingers in the general direction of outside. "It keeps people off balance. It keeps them in awe. You must have noticed how the tourists flock here."

"We have tourists, yes, but you hate them. You've told me that yourself."

"Of course I hate them. But they pay the expenses. How would you like to be without servants?"

"I had an excellent servant. You fired her."

"Yes, I did."

"First Cole. Now Anna."

"I had to make an example."

"You realize you fired my only friends."

"You were being distracted. I need your undivided attention."

"Well, you just lost it."

"But surely," he says, laying his arm along the back of the sofa, "you know these people are not worthy of you. Gypsies? A carpenter's boy? Please!"

"Uncle," I say, "if they're not worthy, neither am I."

"You're a Thummel."

"Everybody tells me that, as though it's some great thing."

"It *is* a great thing."

"Do Thummels value friendship?"

"They value duty. That's more important."

"Then maybe I'm not a Thummel. Not worthy to help you in your rooftop laboratory. You should get someone else."

I watch his face for a reaction. Maybe the tiniest

flinch. I've nicked him where it hurts. "You're making a mistake," he says grimly.

"I don't think so. Now, if you don't mind, I'd like a little privacy so I can take a bath."

"Yes." He pushes himself to his feet. "I can see you must need one, considering where you've been."

I take a deep breath. Then another.

I close the door behind him and lock it. I wish I could lock it twice.

First Elwyn, then Cole, now Anna. Is there anybody left I can talk to? Miss Porlock? There's the teapot. I pick it up and find there's still some tea left. Where's the cup?

I look around, trying to remember where I left it. Before I saw Anna from the window, I set the cup down. Where? Ah yes, on the table. On the *black glass* on the table. The glass is where I left it, but where's the cup?

An awful suspicion sweeps over me.

Okay, a housemaid may have cleaned up and taken it, but maids hardly ever come in the evening. I race around the room looking everywhere it isn't, in order not to accept the obvious: *the cup has disappeared!*

It's the one test Uncle Asa didn't think to make: place something on the mirror and then do nothing.

I pick up Cole's little carved horse. *No, I wouldn't want to lose that. How about this?* I place a perfume bottle in the center of the glass. I never liked the scent anyway. I pull up a chair.

Nothing.

More nothing.

Maybe a slight something. A sort of fizz. Tiny points of light circle the bottle, like bubbles from champagne. Elementals!

More points of light by the moment. A swarm! I back away.

Fewer lights now and less of the bottle. Tiny places where the bottle simply isn't, as if it were riddled with holes. Is this an illusion or some kind of physics I never heard of? The last bubbles blink out, and the mirror lies empty as an abandoned skating rink. Only the slightest scent of perfume lingers in the air.

Try something else! What about this silver letter opener? No one writes to me anyway. I lay it on the glass and hunch down so I'm at eye level with it.

Come on.

Nothing.

Do something!

Finally, it starts. So it works on metal, too. Two, five, a dozen points of light begin to glow.

More appear, a circling constellation.

Then they start blinking out. A minute later, the letter opener is not there. Not anywhere!

I'm struck by the awful finality of Mother's absence. *She disappeared into the mirror, and then the mirror broke.* It's the only explanation that makes sense, the only reason she couldn't meet me that night at the boat. She's *trapped* in there!

How do I get her out?

I pace around the room like an animal. In front of

the window, I stop and stare out at the night, my breath coming in gulps, like sobs without tears.

Maybe I will *take that bath.*

When the tub's full, I step in and sink up to my chin, letting my thoughts drift and my bones relax. *Come on, we can think our way through this.*

Mother. Mirror.

Did the glass *make* her disintegrate, through some unknown chemical action? Or did she pass *through* it, the way my hand passes through the surface of the bathwater? I can still see my hand. If the glass weren't black, could I see my mother? Is she on the other side? Is she *looking out*?

I jump out of the tub, sloshing water, and pad to the table to retrieve the shard of mirror. Back in the bath, I hold it up, but can't see anything, not even myself.

I do feel something, though, or imagine I can. A slight pull, a weak magnetic field, a tingling in my thumb where I'm holding the glass.

Tiny lights begin circling my thumbnail. For a moment, I'm too shocked to move. More points of light, like tiny fireflies.

No! NO!

I let go, and the glass splashes into the water. I'm staring at my thumb.

At most of my thumb.

No blood. Nothing. The top joint of my thumb! *It's not there!*

Chapter Seventeen

"Cole!"

He doesn't hear me.

"Cole! Up here!"

Finally, he looks up. I wave. *"Hold on!"* In my hurry to get down to him, I manage to scrape my knee on the seawall, tearing my skirt. So what—I've got to see him, got to tell him what happened! I make it to the weed-slimed rocks, then pick my way to the sandy beach, where he stands, a half-filled sack slung over his shoulder.

Say something!

Now that I'm in front of him, I can't find the words. I haven't seen Cole since Asa fired him. Are we still friends? I *have* to tell him about the black mirror, but what if he's repulsed? I'm a little repulsed myself. Part of me is *missing*!

I slip the hand in my pocket. "So." Clear my throat. "Where are you headed?"

He squints into the sunrise. How nicely the light slants across the side of his smile! "Nowhere special."

"Mind if I tag along?"

We walk silently, Cole scuffing in his bare feet while I get sand in my shoes. He doesn't notice the soft clicking sound in my pocket as I gently tap the wooden turtle he made me.

Tap it with my glass-tipped thumb!

Click-click. Click.

That was the second shock, as bad as the first. Not just what's missing, but what replaced it: a slant of black glass where the last joint of my thumb used to be—the same glass the mirror's made of. No wonder I couldn't sleep last night. My left hand felt so foreign. Even now I can't stop touching it, and each time I do is a surprise.

Heal it! I told myself. *You can heal wounds, can't you?*

But I couldn't. I tried for half an hour, but no matter how tightly I held the thumb, no matter how hard I concentrated, nothing changed. Finally, I realized: *It isn't a wound. It's an absence. How do you heal what isn't there?*

It may not be there, but I can feel it. In fact, if I don't look straight at it, I'd swear my thumb is whole. Especially when it aches.

Aches to exist.

I hate to think what might've happened if I'd left my hand there longer. Or if the piece of glass were larger. I might've been left with a stump at the end of my wrist!

Click-click. Click-click.

I look over at Cole. "What have you been up to, since—"

"Mostly looking for work."

"Your dad finished those chairs, I see."

"Now he's looking, too. Not much work to be had these days. Not even at the glass factory."

I'm quiet for a while. "I'm sorry you lost your job."

He grunts in agreement.

"He fired my friend Anna, too."

"I know. Nicolae told me. He's not a big fan of your family."

I nod, and we walk on. Ahead of us, along the bluff, stand the wagons of the Gypsies.

Anna, Nicolae, Hanzi. Just thinking about them makes my stomach tighten.

As we pass the docks, fishermen give Cole friendly waves. One of them shouts, "Who's the new girlfriend?"

Cole laughs. Doesn't notice my blush, thank goodness. Everybody knows Cole. Sailors. Gypsies. Shopkeepers. A gaggle of girls passes us, giggling. The tall one with waist-length hair flashes Cole a smile. That red lipstick doesn't suit her at all.

Should I be wearing makeup? Would Miss Porlock allow it?

Should I tilt my head as I talk?

The girl pauses to murmur something to Cole that I can't hear, then flitters away, glancing back as she goes.

"She's pretty," I say.

I bet she has all ten fingers.
No freckles, either.
"She is."
"Do you like her?"
"Sure."

This is so obviously not my business. What I really want to do, what I *have* to do, is tell him about my thumb, which has begun to ache again.

My whole insides are aching, full of sore feelings. I'm not part of Cole's world. I'm this strange creature. I don't even have a parent. Or part of my body.

My thumb twitches.

"What's that clicking sound?" Cole says, pausing.

"What sound?"

"Wait. It stopped."

Should I tell him? I can't. I've got to. Still, I don't say anything. It's like my throat has closed off. "How's your sister?" I say at last.

"Gwen? She's great. She has a birthday coming up. I've been working on her present."

"You keep track of your sister's birthdays?"

He gives me an odd look. "Of course. What do you do at your house?"

Click-click.

"There it is again!"

"There what is?"

"That clicking sound."

I've got to stop doing that. "So," I say, "what are you getting her?"

"I'm building her a kite. It's a new design I've—" He breaks off.

"What?"

"I'm hearing it again."

My breathing slows to nothing. "You mean . . . this?"

He stares as, slowly, I draw my left hand from my pocket.

He takes hold of it and turns it back and forth. "Good God! What *happened*?"

Even I can't believe what I see, and I've been looking at it since last night. Tears fill my eyes. A warm drop lands on his wrist.

Cole's eyes narrow. "Did *he* do this?"

"You mean Uncle Asa?" I shake my head. "I managed it all by myself."

"That's crazy. You would never—"

"Remember in Mother's room? We talked about the black mirror? Well, I have a piece of it. I was holding it, and . . ."

My throat strangles with tears. I look at Cole desperately—glimpse pain in his eyes as he reaches out his arms and enfolds me. He holds me a long time, muffling the world till all I can hear are his bumping heart and the muted screams of seabirds.

Chapter Eighteen

Friend.

I'm getting used to the sound of it.

Seeing my mutilated thumb the other day shocked Cole, but didn't scare him off. That tells a lot about him. Good things.

Now that I've stopped helping Uncle Asa with those foul-smelling experiments, I have more time for myself. Against his wishes (but what isn't?), I've been spending my days outside—with Cole.

Yesterday was interesting. It was Gwen's birthday, and I got to meet the whole Havens clan. Cole led the way to the edge of a slope where the dune grass changes to scrub pine on the way down to the firth. "Here we are."

I didn't see anything but a decrepit wharf sticking out

in the water. Above it, someone long ago had built a sort of house.

Is that where Cole lives?

As we got closer, I heard squeals of children and sounds of running feet; but before we could reach the door, our way was blocked by an explosive orange cat that leaped onto the doorstep, his back arched and eyes glaring. He hissed. Then, with a flick of his tail, he turned and stalked off.

I looked at Cole. "He hissed at me!"

"That," he said, laughing, "was Melon Ball. It's how he says hello."

"I'd hate to find out how he says goodbye."

"Good mouser, though."

"He probably *scares* the poor things to death."

Cole pulled open the door, and a girl in a fluffy dress ran right into him. "Whoa! Slow down, Gwennie."

She broke away and ran, all knees and elbows, after a boy with a balloon.

The party speeded up from there. Cole steered me to the kitchen, where a solid, ruddy-faced woman in a smock was holding a tray of cookies over her head, to keep it from the reaching children.

"Hey, you little monsters," she pleasantly scolded, "these are for later!"

She caught sight of me, and the smile faded. "This is the one?"

Cole nodded. "Mom, this is Cisley."

Mrs. Havens looked me over like I was a suspect cut

of meat. I could guess what she was thinking: *What is my son doing with the spoiled girl from the castle?*

"Hi, Mrs. Havens."

She nodded briefly.

"Can I help?"

"No need," she said, and swept past, just as a large man with a sea captain's beard emerged with packages in one hand and a cane in the other.

"You must be Cisley," he said in an overriding voice. He shifted the packages to his cane side and held out a hand. "I'm Charlie Havens, Cole's father."

His handshake was warm and rough, his eyes blue. "Can I help?" I asked. My second try with that question.

"Could you take these things? They go on the table at Gwen's place."

It wasn't hard to tell which place was hers, her plate surrounded by ribbons and paper-doll cutouts.

Soon everyone was called to table—there was even a plate brought for me—and shouts and laughter rang through the room. I found it a little alarming. I'm never around children and don't know how to talk to them. It's not anything like talking to Uncle Asa.

After cookies and cider came the songs. Oh, the songs. Everybody joined in, as best they knew how, with a round about the bells of London, and another wishing Gwen to live to a thousand and three. I didn't know any of these, but with Cole's nudging, I hummed and stumbled through a verse or two.

Then Mr. Havens stood at the table's head, waited for quiet, and in a strong, mournful voice sang out the old Scottish tune:

What tho' on hamely fare we dine,
Wear hoddin-gray, an' a' that;
Gie fools their silks, and knaves their wine,
A man's a man for a' that.

The table was silent for a bit; then a boy burped, and everyone laughed, and it was time for presents. The one from Gwen's parents turned out to be an oversized story-book with color illustrations. The book was not new, but Gwen received it with gasps of delight.

How did I ever think she was old enough to be Cole's girlfriend? She's taller than most eleven-year-olds, certainly taller than her friends, but she acts younger.

And worships her brother.

Even more so after Cole pulled out his present: a spectacular kite, a big blue trapezoid on which he'd painted a seagull in flight. The idea, he explained to her, was that, on a clear day, the kite would disappear (blue against blue), and all you'd see was the bird.

Gwen jumped up and down, and begged to go out and try it *right now*!

The parents stayed behind while Gwen, Cole, and I trooped outside, along with Gwen's school friends. For the next hour, we ran ourselves ragged up and down the beach while the big white bird sailed overhead. It was exhausting fun, and when I at last headed home, dawdling along the shore, I kept thinking about that family—as poor as beach sand—and about my own.

Today's a different adventure. Cole and I have been clamming, of all things. Something it would never occur to me to do. If I wanted clams, I'd reach for the bellpull and order some, missing all the sunburn and backache of crouching down and digging in wet sand.

It's warmer than usual today as we tramp barefoot along the tidal flats with buckets, trowels, and clamming rake. What a relief to pull off those awful shoes and the itchy stockings beneath. Miss Porlock would have a fit if she saw me, but how else are you supposed to kneel in sand or run through waves?

By early afternoon, Cole and I have filled two buckets. Strolling along, he lugs the pails while I carry the trowels, swinging my shoes. I don't know when I've felt such easy contentment—a warming sun on my face, my new friend beside me.

"Thought I'd drop in on Underwood," he says. "Want to come? He's been having a hard time lately."

"Who's he?"

"You know. He's that painter."

My breath suddenly catches.

"What's the matter?" Cole says.

Click-click. Click-click.

He gives me a closer look. "What is it, Cis?"

"I've seen that man before."

"Of course you have. He's out here every morning with his paints."

"No, I mean somewhere else."

Cole nods toward the bluff. "Well, he lives in that little place up there."

"What do you know about him?"

"Underwood? He's not doing so well these days. Can't find buyers for his work. Who has money for paintings?"

We continue scuffing along.

"My dad's trying to find him a job, anything. Maybe at the glass factory. Of course, he needs a job himself." He gives the buckets a shake, and the shells softly clatter. "I'd like to drop off some of these clams. Some for you, too, of course."

We climb the bluff to the painter's cabin. A board's missing on the weather side, and the shingles look rotted.

Cole knocks.

We wait. He knocks again. "Mr. Underwood?"

He looks at me. "Maybe we should go in. He's got an ice chest where I can put these."

"I don't know. I mean, if he's not home—"

"It's okay. I've been here lots of times."

"He won't get mad?"

Cole is already inside.

It feels silly to stand out here, so I follow, watching as Cole throws open the shutters. Sunlight streams in, revealing, well, I'd call it squalor, but then, I live in a castle, with gleaming corridors and space everywhere. Here, there is space nowhere. Just a paint-spattered counter, a small coal stove, clothes and paint-smeared rags piled on the only chair, a rumpled bed in semi-darkness against the back wall. What strikes me most are the paintings, a dozen canvases, landscapes mostly, covering the narrow walls.

"They're good," I murmur, leaning over to look. I hadn't expected them to be good.

Cole opens the ice chest and empties half a bucket of clams into it, then a little more. "He used to be pretty well-known around here."

"He was?"

"He did that painting of your mom that's in her bedroom."

"He did *that*?"

"I saw the signature."

I flip through some canvases leaning against the wall. I hold one up to see it better: the portrait of a man, pensive, staring out a window. A self-portrait, I realize, an Underwood by Underwood. Am I sure I've seen that face before? I stare at it, trying to think.

After a minute or so, I notice several bright gnats circling the left side of the canvas. It takes a few seconds for me to realize, and then believe, that they're not gnats at all, but points of light—*elementals!* I thump the canvas down, but too late. There's a small, perfectly round hole in the painting.

Cole catches the look on my face. "What is it?"

"My thumb!"

"Your what?" He comes over.

"I keep forgetting. I've put holes in my towels, in my dresses. . . ."

"I don't un—"

"The glass on my thumb!" I cry. "It's the same as the mirror!" Even I can hear the despair in my voice. "Look, I've put a hole in his painting!"

"You're right."

"He's going to hate me."

"I don't know about that. But we've got to be more careful."

Inwardly I thank him for that *we*, like he's part of whatever happens. But I'm the one who has to be careful. I've got to learn to do everything with my other fingers. "It's just lucky," I say, "I haven't caused more damage."

"Well, now we know."

I take a deep breath and nod.

He gives me a one-armed hug. "So. I'm ready if you are."

"Okay." I'm turning to go when a different painting catches my eye. It shows the seawall below the castle, sunlight buttering the edges of rocks and gilding the hair of a distant figure facing out over the firth.

"Hey! That's me!"

Cole looks over my shoulder. "Think so?"

The figure is too far away to make out the features,

but the painting next to it leaves no doubt. It shows me much closer, standing on the wall, shading my eyes with one hand and holding a golden chain in the other—a chain attached to a lobster!

"My God! All these mornings I was watching him, he was watching *me*!"

"I suppose I was watching you, too."

"That's different." I stare hard at the painting. "Come on. Let's get out of here."

We climb down to the beach. By the water, Cole turns to me. "You don't have to worry about Underwood. He's all right."

"How do you know he's all right?"

"Well . . . ," Cole considers.

"And what's he doing here? When did he get to Ravensbirk?"

"A few months ago. Does it matter?"

"I don't know. Maybe not."

"Maybe you should talk to him."

The idea shakes me. But sooner or later, I'm going to have to talk to him about the painting I ruined. "Will you go with me?"

"Sure." His hand reaches up and touches my hair, as if stroking a nervous cat. Then, slowly, he leans forward— *What is he doing?*—and kisses the top of my head! "See you tomorrow?"

I nod dumbly and watch him go.

My brain's in a tumult as I turn toward home. Underwood's paintings. Cole's kiss. All right, it was on the top of my head, but still . . .

Up ahead, the dark rocks rise, and above them, glittering in afternoon light, the castle of glass. The top is almost blinding, as if on fire, flinging brilliant colors in all directions.

As I approach, a cloud slides over the sun, dropping the temperature and extinguishing the light show. For that moment, I see the parapet clearly and a distant figure looking out from it.

I have to shield my eyes to be sure. It's Asa! He's staring at me through field glasses. A shudder runs through me. First, the painter is spying on me. Now it's my uncle. Who else is out there?

I'm being watched. I'm being watched all the time!

Chapter Nineteen

I don't want to go where I'm going, but there it stands, towering above me. The sun's back out, scattering rainbows and turning the castle into a prism.

A prison.

I'm grateful for this stretch of beach before the climb to the seawall. A few more minutes of freedom, sand warm between my toes. I wonder if Asa is still up there spying on me. Of course he is. I'm not going to look.

I'd rather look at the mirage the sun is making on the wet sand up ahead. The beach is a blinding shimmer. In the midst of it stands a tiny point of darkness.

Curious.

The trembling light recedes as I walk, but the object remains.

A shell! A beautiful conch shell. Turning it in my hand,

I'm sure I've never seen one so perfect: off-white at its widest, threaded round with delicate brown lines, then turning coral as it spirals to a point. I've got to take this home with me!

You're supposed to hear the ocean, aren't you? Up to my ear. Nothing. I give it a shake and try again. What's wrong with this thing?

I speak into it. "Hello?"

Immediately there's an echo: "Hello . . . hello . . ."

"Hello!" I say louder.

"Hello! . . . Hello! . . . lo! . . . lo . . ."

This is kind of fun.

"How did you get here?"

"Get here . . . ere . . . ere . . ."

"Who's in there?" I demand, smiling.

Silence.

Silence? Where's the echo? "Is anybody *there*?" I give the shell a shake.

Again, no echo. What happened?

"Of course I'm here," a quiet voice replies.

I yank the shell away from me. *I didn't hear that!*

Glance around. Not a soul. With a trembling hand, I lift the shell again. "Did you say something?"

"Smart girl."

I almost drop it.

"Wh-who are you?"

"Not important."

"Not *important*?"

"Just wind in an empty shell."

The voice is like my own, a bit lower, with a ragged undertone, as if it came from a cavern. Is it my imagination? This reminds me of Elwyn, my little lobster friend. Everyone thought I was imagining *him* speaking to me.

But he *was* speaking. Wasn't he?

I turn the shell around. Examine all angles. This has got to be a trick. I'm used to magic tricks and good at figuring them out.

"Do you know who I am?" I say finally.

No answer.

"I said, do you know—?"

"You're a lonely girl who can use someone to talk to."

I forget to breathe.

"You don't suppose I talk to every beachcomber who comes along," it continues.

I don't know *what* to suppose. Instead, I jump to my biggest question: "Do you know Elwyn?"

No reply.

"Elwyn?" I ask again. "He's a lobster."

"Different family entirely."

"Well, I know that, but I just thought—"

There's a brief gusty sound, suspiciously like a sigh. "You'd better take me with you. I have a feeling you're going to need me."

"One more question?"

"What?"

"Are you, you know, empty?"

"Am I what?"

"Isn't there generally a mollusk or something . . . ?"

"You really need to know this?"

"I'd *like* to know."

"I asked her to leave."

"Oh."

"You can't get a decent echo with some fat old mollusk crawling about."

"I suppose not."

"Now," the voice goes on, "you should hurry. Your uncle is not the most patient of men."

"Right." Stomach rumbling—nerves again—I tuck the shell under my arm and climb the rocks to the seawall. *Not the most patient of men.* No, I wouldn't say he was.

Well, who cares? What can he do?

Today, for the first time in weeks, I can enter through the labyrinth. The renovation is finished, or so the pantry maid told me. Let's see what this fancy new maze looks like.

Asa has been secretive about it, not only fixing the machinery, but (I see now) rearranging the whole place—new walls, blind alleys I didn't know about, even a pit filled with what looks like quicksand. He also added several large topiary animals—a hedge in the shape of a wolf, another in the shape of a bear rearing up on hind legs.

I stop, uncertain. I'm not used to feeling lost.

Ah, two hedges away, the gardener stands on a high ladder, clipping one of the taller plantings into a giraffe. He'll know the way.

But I can't ask. *Miss Thummel wants me to show her how to get into her own house.*

"Need help?"

The voice is close by.

I peer around a hedge. Nothing but a thornbush with needlelike spines. "Who's there?"

"Who do you think?" says the voice.

I stare at the conch.

"Stay to the left," it says. "Take the second turning."

"How do you—?" I stop myself and do what I'm told. The path leads to a blind alley.

Before I can say anything: "See that pointed stone? Be a dear and give it a half turn to the right."

Again, I obey. With a loud creak, the hedge opens outward.

"He'll have to put some oil on that," says the voice in the shell. "Now just go ahead, turn right, and you're home."

"Wait!" I say, stopping where I am. "How do you know these things?"

"Not important."

"I'm not taking another step until you tell me."

"Oh my. You're scaring me."

My eyes narrow. "Listen. The labyrinth was just finished today. You weren't anywhere near it."

"Wasn't I?"

I look around. The gardener on his ladder is looking at me oddly.

I lower my voice. "You couldn't be."

"Don't confuse me with the house I live in. I don't confuse you with yours."

I turn the shell around in my hand. It *is* a house, isn't it?

"Do you know where the wind is?" the shell continues.

I shake my head.

"Think of me as a breath inside the wind inside the sky. Can you do that?"

"A breath inside the wind . . . I like that."

"I'm glad."

Soon I'm stepping into the castle's atrium, where I'm met, not by a furious uncle or an officious Strunk, but by a very cross-looking Edna Porlock. She shakes her large head at me. "Cisley Thummel."

Taking hold of my shoulder, she steers me toward the staircase. "No time to clean you up. Your uncle wants to see you right away!"

Chapter Twenty

Windblown as I am, Miss P. presents me to Uncle Asa in his study. It is one of the few darkly furnished rooms in the whole glass palace, with its large captain's desk, leather chairs, and mahogany bookcases.

Asa's a spot of darkness himself. Something's different about him. He looks older, his coat noticeably soiled and his hair disheveled. His hair is *never* disheveled.

How long has it been—a week?—since I've seen him? Either he's been out in the labyrinth or up in the laboratory. He even takes his meals up there. Maybe he *sleeps* there.

Janko, his henchman, has positioned himself by the door, hands clasped behind his back, at ease, but ready. Does he think I'm going to make a break for it?

Click-click.

"Hello, Uncle."

Click-click, click-click.

He leans back in his chair. "I hope," he says quietly, eyes half closed, fingers interlaced on his stomach, "you enjoyed your little jaunt today."

I don't say anything.

"Because it's your last."

"You mean you're going to kill me?"

"I mean you're confined to the castle."

"What?"

"Mezzanine floor only. Your meals will be brought to you."

"I can't believe this!"

"You are restricted for the foreseeable future. The servants are instructed to make sure you stay put."

Janko screws his face into a sort of smile.

"What have I done?"

"What have you done?" Asa murmurs, rubbing his forehead. "Where do I start?"

"I haven't done anything wrong!"

"I was mistaken about you," he says, ignoring my outburst. "I thought you were old enough to understand appropriate behavior. How old are you, anyway? Twelve?"

"I'm thirteen!"

"Thirteen. And yet you continue to gang about with the lowest elements. Just look at you." He twirls a dismissive hand. "You look like the wreck of the *Hesperus*."

"The what?"

"And what are you holding there? Not another verminous pet, I hope."

"It's a seashell!"

He sighs.

I take a slow breath. Arguing will only get me in deeper. "How long," I say quietly, "do you plan to keep me cooped up?"

"Until you learn to behave like a Thummel. There are certain obligations for people like us. Certain proprieties." He sees my expression. "They are *not* to be mocked."

I'm silent. He sits silently as well. I suspect I'm one detail in a long, irritating day. By the doorway, Janko folds his arms. I can't see Porlock without turning around, but I hear her muttering, the way she does.

Be calm, I tell myself. *Plot your escape later.* "Is there any way I can shorten my sentence?"

"Your sentence. You would think of it that way. Well, as it happens," he says, "there may be." His eyes show a bit of their old spark, like he's been just waiting for this: "There's a project I can use some help on in the laboratory."

"Uncle, if you think for one minute—"

"You'd be glad to," a soft voice whispers. Not my voice. Not Miss P.'s.

"If I think for one minute what?" says Asa. "Speak up!"

"You need to help him." Same quiet voice. My God, it's the shell!

"Why should I?" I demand.

140

"Don't take that tone with me, young lady."

"I wasn't talking to you."

"Are you being impertinent?"

"Don't you ever want to walk on the beach again?"

"Of course!"

Asa looks incredulous.

"Then do what he asks."

"I don't think so."

"Oh. Now you don't *know* if you're being impertinent!"

"I'm sorry, Uncle. Did you say something?"

"Get out! You can rot in your room for all I care!"

"No, Asa!" It's Miss Porlock's voice now. She steps beside me and lays an arm around my shoulder. "Can't you
see? She isn't making sense. She's obviously not well."

Uncle Asa peers at me. "Are you not well?"

"I'm fine. It's just confusing with everybody talking
at once."

"Well then, let me put it to you simply," says Asa. "If
you help *me*, I'll help *you*."

Visions of mutilated mice and slivered lizards dance
in my head.

"I know you, Cisley," murmurs the shell. *"I know what
you're thinking."*

"You *think* you know me."

"Whether I do or not is beside the point," says Asa.
"I'm making you an offer. Do you want to help me or
not?"

"You really want to refuse, don't you?"

141

"Yes, I do!"

Asa's face relaxes. "Very good," he says, setting his hands on the chair arms. "Now you're showing some sense."

"No," I say. "Wait."

"How about tomorrow, first thing?"

I glare at the conch shell. "You tricked me."

"Not at all," says Asa. "Tomorrow, then. Janko will fetch you at seven."

Chapter Twenty-One

"What was *that* about?" I'm pacing around the little bed-side table where I've set the shell.

"Just trying to be helpful."

"Helpful!" This is so aggravating I don't know what to say. "Don't you understand? I refuse to have anything to do with that man and his horrible experiments!"

The conch remains silent. A decorative object on a table.

"*Well?*" My fists dig into my hips. "What do you have to say?"

No answer.

"And how do you know so much? How did you know the way through the labyrinth? You don't even have legs!"

"Does the wind have legs?"

"Are you saying you're the wind?"

"It's an expression."

"Well, what *are* you? *Who* are you?"

"I'm a voice."

A soft knock on my door makes me turn. It's Miss Porlock.

She glances around the room. "Who are you talking to?"

"To myself, apparently," I shoot back carelessly.

She peers at the drapes, in case someone's hiding. "You seemed to be having quite an argument."

"I disagree with myself a lot."

"My goodness," she says, seeing the conch. "What a pretty shell! I hadn't really noticed before."

I give it a sour glance. "Looks aren't everything."

Miss P. takes this in, vaguely. "I came," she says, "to see how you were bearing up."

I look at her blankly.

"Your uncle can be a bully," she says, nodding. "But I want you to know you will always have a friend in Edna Porlock." Her eyelids lower in a sunset of kindly wrinkles.

"Thanks. Good to know. Now, can you get me out of here?"

"It's my understanding you'll be free to come and go once you've helped your uncle."

"How long do I have to help him?"

"He didn't say."

"It could be weeks. It could be years!"

Miss P. evidently hadn't thought of that. "I suppose it could." Her eyes wrinkle up again with emotion. "I suspect there's a special reason you'd like your freedom just now. Am I wrong?"

"Special reason?"

A penciled eyebrow rises knowingly. "A special person, perhaps?"

"You mean Cole?"

Her cheeks tremble into a smile. "Is that the boy's name?"

"That's his name, yes." *Patience, Cisley,* I tell myself. "How do you know about Cole? Have you been spying on me?"

"Cisley, really. I would never do that!"

"Everyone else does."

"Well, it's hard not to notice that you've been spending a lot of time with a certain nice-looking boy."

"We were digging clams."

She doesn't seem to know what to do with that information.

"I got a sunburn," I add. "And a backache."

"Love's little sacrifices."

My teeth clench, which is a bad sign, because I really don't want to snap at Miss Porlock. "Well," I say, "if you see Uncle Asa, ask how long he expects to keep me here."

"I will. And I'll visit you every day. We'll make the best of things. Oh," she says, "I have some love poetry in Latin that I think you'll particularly like."

"I'm sure I will."

At the door, she gives me a smile, full of a spinster's wisdom about the ways of the heart.

Alone finally, I realize how much I miss Elwyn. At least he knew how to keep a secret. What on earth do I do with a talkative seashell with a mind of its own?

Next morning, I'm at my window in time to see dawn inching up over the Firth of Before. Far down the beach, a lone figure comes this way. The loping, forward tilt of his stride tells me it's Cole. Yes, today's the day we were going to see the painter, Peter Underwood. Cole doesn't know I won't be coming. I've got to tell him.

He's out of view for a minute as he climbs the rocks to the seawall, then reappears, much closer. His tousled hair catches the light as he takes a seat on our lookout rock, too far away for me to shout to him. I open the window and signal him with wild hand waves, but he's not looking this way.

A knock on the door and the chambermaid, stifling a yawn, brings my breakfast tray—poached eggs and toast under a round silver cloche.

She's new, since Anna left. Body like unbaked dough. Dull eyes, no expression. Bonnie, her name is. "Listen," I tell her. "Do you see that boy down there?"

She peers out. Nods slowly.

"Will you run down and tell him I won't be meeting him today?"

She looks as if I've asked her to fly. "All the way down there?"

"That's right. I can't meet him today or anytime soon."

This girl is no Anna. I end up bribing her with my hairbrush, the one inlaid with ivory. I suspect she'll keep the brush and ignore the errand. Maybe she'll even tell on me.

And I *liked* that brush.

When she's gone, I turn to the shell on the night table. "Why did you tell Uncle Asa I would work with him?"

Long pause. Then a gusty voice, a little lower than my own, replies: "It will be different this time."

"Different? How?"

Whatever my breathy friend is about to say gets interrupted by a loud knock on the door. Not waiting for me to open it, Janko bangs in.

"You are ready, no?"

I glance around. I decide to leave the shell where it is. Who knows what it might decide to blurt out?

"I am ready, yes."

Chapter Twenty-Two

A rotten-egg smell greets me as we reach the roof. It gets abruptly worse when Janko opens the laboratory door and gestures me in.

Click-click-click.

"Um," I say, "maybe this isn't the best time?"

He takes a step toward me.

I duck in, just in time to glimpse an object whiz past my head and crash tremendously against one of the metal supports. Dirt and broken clay fly in all directions, small bits peppering my face. There's Asa, hunched, glaring, his eyes as wild as his hair.

I quickly step out again.

But there's Janko. He grabs my arm and practically flings me inside, slamming the door shut.

Asa looks up at the sound. He's like someone waking from a dream. "You!" he says.

"Uncle, are you all right?"

He runs a sooty hand through his hair. "What are you doing here?"

"You told me to come!"

"Oh." He looks around as if he's misplaced something.

"Are you sure you're all right?"

He doesn't answer.

"Uncle?"

"I haven't been sleeping well."

That makes two of us. "Did you throw that flowerpot at me?"

"At you?" He finally focuses. "Of course not. I didn't see you sneaking about."

"I was not sneak—"

"Glad to hear it." He expels a huffy sigh. "Now, what do you say; shall we get to work?" He fits a vial over a small flame. His lab coat, once white, is blotched with orange stains.

"Uncle Asa, what's that horrible smell?"

"Sulfur. Some so-called expert said sulfur would work. I'm here to tell you it does not."

"Can we at least keep the door open?"

"Can't. Temperature control." He takes a flat metal case from a shelf and unlatches it, revealing scores of stoppered test tubes with labels in Latin. He selects two and sets them on a stand.

"What do you want me to do?" I tap the glass end of my thumb nervously. I don't want him to see it. I don't want anyone to see it.

"Get me down that book. Third from the right? That's it."

It's heavy, but I carry it with one hand, keeping the other out of sight. *Le Vrai Mystère de la Rose Noire*. "It's in French."

He riffles through it, then slaps his hand down. "Where am I supposed to find *that*?"

"Find what?"

"A certain black moss grows in the south of France. In *winter*." He rubs his forehead. "You may have noticed we are not in the south of France. And it is not winter."

"What do you need it for, this moss?"

No reply. He's checking the glass vial over the flame. The liquid inside has turned brown.

"*Damn!*"

"What are you trying to do?"

"The impossible. Now, if you want to be useful as well as ornamental, you could hand me those calipers on the hook there."

"You're still trying, aren't you, Uncle Asa?"

No answer. He wipes the back of his hand across his forehead, leaving a smear.

"But you *know* it can't be done."

Silence.

"Mother had to know that, too."

He pours the vial of brown liquid into the sink.

"Maybe she was teasing you." I'm determined to get a reaction. "Maybe it was a joke."

He whirls around, his eyes murderous. "A *joke*?"

I flinch.

"A *JOKE*?" He bangs the vial down on the counter, shattering the glass.

"I didn't mean *joke*, exactly."

His gaze is iron. "I am doing these experiments," he says, grinding his syllables slowly, "in case it is *not* a joke. In case everybody is *wrong*. In case it is possible after all!"

I step back. My thumb is clicking madly. I've seen that look on his face before. He's jealous. It's that simple. Mother never let him forget he was a fraud: Asa Thummel, master magician, who has no magic in him.

Now she's gone. Now's his chance. No wonder he's throwing flowerpots.

"Uncle," I say, getting my courage up, "why do you want me here?"

"I don't know."

"You don't?"

"I need you in place."

"What makes you think I'd be any use? I'm not a scientist."

"I don't want a scientist. *I'm* the scientist. I need a helper."

"There's Janko."

"Ah yes, there's Janko," he says, with a twist. "Why didn't I think of that?"

"Or any of the other servants, if all you need is someone to fetch your books and sweep up your broken flowerpots."

"*Stop it!*"

I stop.

"I need *you*. You're the only one who can understand what I'm doing here. The only one with *magic*." His dark eyebrows tilt in as he holds me in his gaze. "Not much, as far as I can tell, but you have some. Chemistry alone may not be the answer."

"But," I protest, "*I* can't make you a black rose. We tried that experiment. Several times, as I recall."

"Obviously we were doing something wrong."

"Or else it's really impossible."

"Maybe. Or maybe the right chemicals—I haven't given up on chemistry, you see. In fact . . ." He lurches over to the stand of test tubes. "In fact," he says, "you might want to take a look at this. It's one of my small successes."

"What is it?"

"Co-pigmentation."

"What?"

"In this tube, we have a colorless flavonoid. In this other one, we have a combination of cyanidins."

Is he purposely trying to confuse me?

"Colorless chemicals," he explains. "But combine them, and you can change the appearance of a pigment."

"I'm afraid Miss Porlock's chemistry lessons—"

"It simply means you can change the color. That's how I got that rose." He points to one of the plants.

I stare at it. "It's blue."

"You're observant."

"I thought you were making a black rose."

"I had to do something that's possible before trying something that's impossible. I had to come up with a method."

"And have you?"

"We'll see." Then, more softly, to himself, "We'll see."

I stare at the rose, then at Asa. Sometimes, like now, my uncle seems perfectly sane. Other times, quite mad.

What will he be five minutes from now?

Chapter Twenty-Three

An hour later, no closer to success, he excuses me for the day. Janko sits on the parapet, gazing out, smoking a vile cigar. He doesn't turn as I pass.

I dawdle down the staircase to my room, a thumb click for every step.

Trapped. Tricked. Stuck.

I did what the shell told me to. I need to have a word with that bag of wind. There it sits on my bedside table, looking innocent.

"I suppose you know what went on upstairs," I say. "You seem to know everything else."

No response.

"Don't pretend you don't hear me."

I might as well be talking to a chair leg.

"Fine. I'm leaving." I head to the door, but pause.

Where do I think I'm going? Not outside. Not downstairs. If I don't help my uncle, I'm confined to this floor, pretty much forever.

"Actually . . ." The voice is quiet.

I turn. "Did you say something?"

"Actually, I don't understand him any more than you do. What he's doing up there doesn't make sense."

"I know. All he did was turn a flower blue."

"It's sad."

"He thinks if he can get the right chemicals—"

A little gust from the shell. Disgust? Some other kind of gust?

"What is it?" I ask.

"I'm going to have to help him."

I pick the shell up. "And how do you propose to do that?"

"Not so loud. You don't have to talk right into the opening."

I can't believe this. I'm being scolded by a seashell! I set it down.

"Come on," says the voice. "Let's forget all this. Go for a walk."

"We can't."

"I don't mean outside. Follow our noses. Well, your nose."

When I step into the hall, the shell under my arm, my nose does give me a hint: the smell of flowers: Mother's room.

We set off. My uncle has made the corridors more

complicated today, the better to keep me from wandering, I suppose. That's quite apart from the Mirror Maze. Gradually, mirror by sliding panel, the scent grows stronger, until I find myself outside my mother's door.

I don't have a key.

I look at the lock, then at my thumb, the slant of black glass at the end of it.

At the lock again.

Can't hurt to try. Gently, I press my thumb against the lock and hold it there.

A few seconds of nothing at all. More seconds of nothing at all. Finally, after more than a minute, two tiny pinpoints ignite. Then three more flecks. They circle. The lock brightens. Before long, hundreds of lights swarm the lock, so bright I can't look at them directly.

But then I see fewer of them. Fewer and fewer.

I pull my thumb away. Where the lock had been, there is now a neat thumb-sized hole. I give the door a push, and it swings open.

"Well done," says the shell.

On the mantel, a white rose dimly gleams. I place the shell beside it and feel my way through the sitting room to the red-tinged gloom of the bedroom, where the portrait of Mother hangs. I stand before it, my vision adjusting to the half-light, and stare into her eyes. I realize we share something, a secret no one else understands. I don't understand it myself, but know it would be lost if I pulled open the drapes and let in the brutal logic of daylight.

The sheen of her gown catches my eye, reminding me of the closet and its treasures.

Go ahead, says a voice in my head.

Maybe I will, I mentally reply.

The closet door swings open as I approach. Somehow that seems natural, and I sweep in as if I belong here. It's also natural that I can see where I'm going, with no lamps or windows. A twilight glimmer comes from the dresses themselves, long rows of them brushing against me on either side, welcoming me, reaching out to me, although I've never worn such clothes in my life. Never wanted to, before I discovered the wonders of this closet. Now I can't get enough of them.

That red silk dress, for instance, floor-length, low in the back. It's wonderfully daring, with its single shoulder strap. Too long for me, too full, I can see that, but so soft!

Nobody's looking. Go ahead.

I pull it down and run out to the bedroom. Before the mirror, I slip it over my head and smooth the material over my hips. Immediately, it forms itself perfectly to my body. Is this really me? I feel like a red tulip, tightly petaled.

"Need any help?" I hear from the other room.

I'd forgotten about the shell.

"Isn't it fantastic?" I say, turning around before it.

The shell considers. "The fit's perfect. But . . ."

"What?"

"Who does your hair, that Porlock woman?"

"I do. What's wrong?"

"Sit down. I'll talk you through it."

I take the chair at the vanity. "We're going to need more light," I say, and reach for the crystal match strike. But before I can light the table lamp, the shell shushes me.

Someone is outside the door, going through keys, then stopping, realizing there's no lock.

"Hide!" the shell hisses.

I grab my clothes and race to the closet, easing the door shut behind me. All I can think is that Asa—or worse, Janko—has come to drag me back to the lab.

Crawling between dresses, I crouch behind a ball gown. The outside door creaks open.

A long silence, then footsteps, muffled by the Oriental rug.

The shell! I left it out there!

Maybe he won't notice.

I hear a scratching sound, then smell a match. A faint light flimmers.

After a long minute, a drawer groans open. Bumps shut.

Then another drawer.

A thief! Do we have thieves in the castle?

The steps come closer, then stop. I close my left hand in a fist, but leave my thumb free, careful not to touch anything. The doorknob turns. My breath halts. Then a light darts about, making sequins wink.

The footsteps are coming right toward me! Trying to

shrink back, I brush against a taffeta dress, which makes a shushing sound.

The steps cease. Someone is listening.

I listen to him listening.

The steps resume. Pass next to me. A shock: thumping by are the brown, thick-heeled shoes I've seen so often before.

Not Asa after all. Not Janko.

Edna Porlock! What's she doing here?

My old tutor turns and stumps back out to the bedroom.

I wait a long minute, a muddle of confusion—*Miss Porlock!*—then creep from my hiding place and peek through the narrow opening by the door hinge. Now Miss P. is going through Mother's bureau. She slides open the top drawer, contemplates what she sees there, pulls something out. Turns and holds it up: a pair of filmy silk stockings.

She gives it a long look, holds it to her cheek, feeling its softness. Her eyes close.

I shouldn't be seeing this.

The lamplight flashes on something metallic, turning it gold. Scissors! Slowly, as if dreaming, Miss Porlock snips the stockings in half.

She continues cutting until the bureau top is littered with silken fragments. She stares at what she has done, her face a mask. Now she gathers the remnants, sweeps them back in the drawer, and closes it.

She lifts her chin, checks her hair in the mirror, and walks out of my range of sight.

With a creak, the outer door opens, then bumps shut.

When I'm sure she's gone, I quick-change my clothes, and grab the shell from the mantel.

"Let's get out of here!"

Chapter Twenty-Four

"Sheep manure?"

"That's what it says. Three teaspoons."

My nose, my eyes, and any other part of me that can wrinkle wrinkles. The curse of a sensitive nose. At least it's *dry* manure. I measure it into the vial.

"Now," says Asa, reading, "the powdered alder fruit."

"How much?"

He flips the page back and forth. "It doesn't say. What idiot wrote this? It's no good unless you know the measurement!"

I wait. I've learned that Uncle Asa has to finish ranting before he can listen.

"Two months I waited for that shyster bookseller in Calais! And the book is useless!"

I wait.

"He's supposed to know his business!"

His anger is winding down. Good.

"What if we make three batches," I suggest, "with different amounts? Maybe one will be right."

"You have to be exact."

"What choice do we have?"

He sighs.

Three batches are made, turned into paste by an admixture of vinegar and salt, and applied to the stripped roots of three rosebushes.

He looks at me. "Do you think it will work?"

"Well, we've got three chances that it will."

"Be honest."

"No, I don't."

We've been at this six days now, trying everything he can think of in every book he has. We even talk at dinner. That's new. We discuss grafting methods. I back off when he yells, but lately he's been yelling at others, including some long-dead botanists.

Privately? None of these experiments will work. He's trying to create a magical plant through mechanical means.

But I'm willing to help. Sooner or later, it will gain me my freedom; and it allows me to nose around for clues to Mother.

Two days after the sheep manure experiment, the plants are dying. But ever resourceful, we try a new method of grafting: we attach the roots of a rose to the stem of a black currant bush and, in a separate experiment, to a black birch sapling. Grafting has never been tried like this.

We're almost finished when the door swings open. Mr. Strunk stands there, a stubby silhouette, holding a package. His nose twitches. He should have *my* smelling ability. "Something for you, sir," he says.

Asa doesn't look up. "See what it is," he tells me. "I didn't order any more books."

I wrestle open the packaging. "It's a book, all right. An old one. I think it's in Latin."

He frowns. "What's the matter with your thumb?"

I try to ignore the stab of panic. After all, I've been careful to keep my thumb out of sight for weeks.

"Nothing. I cut myself."

His look narrows. "Wait. I happen to know you can heal cuts."

I pause a little too long.

"I think you're lying. Let me see it."

I try to pull away, but he catches my wrist. My glass thumb tip gleams like a lighthouse. He turns my hand back and forth, his eyes intent. He taps the glass tip. "What on God's earth . . . ?"

I take a deep breath. "I found a piece of the mirror. You'd thrown it out."

"The black mirror? You *stole* it?"

"You'd thrown it *out*!"

"Never mind. What happened to the thumb?"

I blow out a sigh. "Can we sit down?"

"No, we cannot sit down. What happened?"

There's no way to avoid this. Before I'm finished telling him, he has stopped listening. "Where's the glass now?" he demands. "Get it. Bring it here."

Not a word about how I feel, or what it might be like to be a girl with a partly amputated thumb.

I head downstairs and retrieve the glass from the back of my closet. I'm careful to hold it from underneath, by its lead backing.

Asa pushes the new book aside and lays the mirror on the table. "I'd given up on this thing." He shakes his head. "Let's see what we can find out." He reaches into a terrarium, pulls out a wriggling chameleon, and sets it on the glass.

The lizard looks up at me.

"Wait!" I say. "Take something else. This pencil."

"I want to see if it works on a living organism."

"It does! Just look at my thumb!"

"Be quiet. It's starting."

The slightest fizz of light begins circling the bewildered creature. The lights grow clearer, more numerous, while the chameleon loses bits of itself. Instead of changing from one color to another, as such creatures do, it changes from something into nothing.

Then it's gone.

Asa picks up the mirror, turns it upside down, and shakes it.

"Do you think he'll fall out?" I ask.

"I don't know what I think. I think it's magic."

"Be careful how you hold that," I add hastily. "Hold it from underneath."

He sets the glass down. "So." His gaze is intense. "We're left with a dilemma. It seems that in order to *make* magic, we have to *have* magic."

"Probably true."

"Which is one definition of *impossible*."

We look at each other in silence.

I raise my eyebrows.

He lowers his.

Chapter Twenty-Five

Somehow, I expect Miss Porlock to look different. I certainly look at her differently. It makes me nervous just sitting across from her. But here she is, in her usual seat by the window, biting into a ginger cookie and going over notes for today's lesson. Not a trace of the furtive creature in the dark, pawing through Mother's things.

This afternoon, it's history. English. From Thomas Cromwell all the way to Oliver Cromwell. Lots of torture and burnings at the stake. Somehow it feels appropriate.

I dip one of her cookies in my tea in hopes of softening it and write dutifully in my notebook, but it's hard to concentrate. When Miss P. speaks of the beheading of Anne Boleyn, all I can think about is a dark room and the flash of scissors.

An hour in the court of Henry VIII has worn out even

Miss Porlock. She releases me, and I step into the hall, the conch shell under my arm. Voices of tourists reach me from the atrium—the afternoon group. No one up here, thank goodness, although they'll be brought up later to be shown the Mirror Maze, Uncle Asa's pride.

Free to wander, I head for Mother's rooms. I've been going there a lot these days. It's my secret, a place where I don't have to be polite or obedient or normal. A place that understands me.

Arriving at her door, I have a little shock: the lock has been replaced—in fact, with a larger, stronger lock than before. I suppose Strunk is responsible, no doubt instructed by Asa.

I smile. Do they really think they can keep me out, when the answer's at the tip of my thumb? Three minutes later, the lock doesn't exist, and the door sways open.

Dimness, silence, the sweet scent of a white rose on the mantel.

Ordinarily, that's where I'd leave the shell, but today I take it to the vanity. It has been giving me advice on hair, something I never gave a thought to in my younger days—three weeks ago. Why am I so interested now? And dresses! I used to hate dresses.

"Can you help me do my hair like Mother in the painting?"

A breathy voice: "I'm afraid your tutor would not approve."

That gets a giggle out of me. "No, I don't suppose she would."

"Too adult?"

I pick up the shell. "You don't like her, do you?"

"Me? I'm nothing. Just a gust of wind."

"So you say."

"Shall we start? First, brush your hair out so we see what we have to work with."

I settle myself at the vanity and watch my image in the three-sided mirror. An arsenal of Mother's implements lies before me, and during the next twenty minutes I use most of them. When we're finished, the Cisley before me looks more eighteen than thirteen, her long brown hair swept upward in carefully casual swells, like waves on the verge of breaking.

"What do you think?" says the voice from the shell.

"My goodness!" I jump up and run to compare myself to the painting. In the half-light, Mother gazes down at me, her expression inscrutable. Our hairstyles are identical—identical!—but there's something I'm missing.

Apart from her blazing beauty, of course.

The dress. It must be in the closet.

Go ahead, says a voice inside me. I've been hearing that voice a lot lately. Disobedient. Hard to resist.

The closet door swings open as I approach, and I enter as I would a church. The way ahead is dim as a wedding aisle lit by glowworms. Lines of gowns sway like well-wishers, a fantasy so strong I find myself nodding to each one as I pass.

Go on; go on, they urge, silks rustling.

I've never made it all the way to the back—although I've set out for it twice before—and I begin to wonder if the closet ever ends, or if it's like the images in mirrors reflecting other mirrors, myself, my selves, forever.

I pass the red gown I tried on last time, and farther ahead, the white sheath with the diamonds up the side. I nod to each. Continuing, I hear muffled whispers.

Is someone here?

The sounds, very soft, come from just ahead. They're not in any language I know, unless it's the language of satin. They're coming from, swirling from, circling around, one of the gowns—floor-length, pale blue, the very dress from the portrait!

Reverently, I unhook it and carry it out.

Way too long for me, of course. Way too everything. A daring swoop. Getting into this thing, I realize, will be a project in itself.

I step out of the girlish dress that Porlock likes me to wear, and pause, catching my own eyes in the mirror. *What do I think I'm doing?*

But then that other voice: *Who has a better right?*

I gather the material and slip it over my head, careful about my hair. Immediately, strange as it sounds, the gown takes over. It never touches my hair as it slithers over me, whispering as it goes. I feel caressed, perfumed, as the waist cinches itself, the hem retracts, the bodice conforms to my more modest size. I reach back for the satin buttons and find them already done to the top.

I behold a transformed Cisley Thummel. Heart

pounding, I turn and face the portrait of Mother. A shiver goes through me. For a moment, it's as though I can see through the painting—and she can see me!

All my life, she's been a mystery to me; but maybe I've been a mystery to myself. I look into her eyes and feel some of that same mischief in my own.

Mischief and something else. Something . . . worse?

Asa. Strunk. Porlock. Janko. Not an ounce of magic among them. What makes them think they can tell me how to dress? Or how to behave? I'm not a child anymore. Not here.

I could fool them. I could play tricks on them.

I could hurt them.

My stomach drops. How could I *think* such a thing? But here in this room, it feels . . . thrilling. *We're different from them, Mother. No one makes rules for us.*

We mirror each other.

Oh. Except for one thing. I run to the outer room and fetch the rose from the mantel. Then I stand before Mother and try to hold it the way she's holding hers, the casual assurance, the lightness of touch, the curve of her wrist.

There are still differences. The roses, obviously. Hers is black, as black as Underwood's paintbrush could paint it. Mine is white.

Just then a distant whistle breaks my reverie. Who do I know who whistles like that? I run to the window and pull aside the drape. It's coming from the beach. *Cole!*

I shake myself, shake off Mother and the thoughts I

just had. It's Cole! He puts his fingers to his lips and lets out another long whistle. He's looking toward the castle. Toward my room.

I push open the window. "Here! I'm up here!"

I wave frantically, but I'm in the other wing and he's not looking this way.

Not thinking, I run out in the corridor. One of the new cleaning women looks up from the statue she's been dusting. She stares at me, her mouth agape, like a hooked fish.

Before she can speak, I thrust the rose in her hand and run past into the Mirror Maze.

A group of tourists is shuffling along ahead of me, led through the maze by their energetic guide. I slip in among them. At first, no one notices, and together we start down the curving glass staircase to the atrium. I try to keep my head down, while looking out for Janko and Strunk; but my head is gorgeously not my own, and my body a river of satin. Several people have become aware of me. They turn and stare, but seem afraid to say anything.

Trying to hide is not going to work.

Be a Thummel, I tell myself. And I stand erect, chin up. *Be Marina!*

Now everyone steps aside, practically tripping over themselves to make way for me. "It's her!" gasps an elderly woman, laying her hand on her throat.

A girl whispers to her friend, "It's the magic lady. The one who was killed!"

We reach the atrium, and I separate myself from the

others, hurrying toward the kitchen and back exit. Mrs. Quay glances up at me from the meat pie she's readying for the oven, and for a moment I see fear in her eyes.

Then I'm outside in the wind.

I'm running.

PART THREE

A Quiet Lie

Chapter Twenty-Six

My heart's thumping hard, not just from running. We haven't seen each other in weeks, and I haven't been able to explain to him why. Did that serving girl ever give Cole the message that I couldn't meet him?

The first thing he says confuses me. "What *happened* to you?"

I stand before him, catching my breath. "What do you mean? Oh." Only now do I remember the gown. The satin shoes. The hair.

Oh, the hair!

"Tell me later," he says. "You can still heal people, right?"

"What?"

"I need your help. Somebody's hurt."

"Hurt? How?"

"Let's walk. In fact, can you run?" He grabs hold of my hand and pulls me to a trot.

"Wait!" I stop and take off Mother's satin pumps. Barefoot, I can run fast, but it's still hard to keep up. After a minute, my breath is ragged.

"What happened?" I manage.

"Accident. The glass factory."

I remember something about that factory, the only one in Ravensbirk. Started by Uncle Asa years ago to make glass for his castle. "Is it very bad?"

Would Cole be running if it weren't?

"Do you have a doctor?" I ask, breathing hard.

"Who can afford a doctor?" He glances over, sees me gulping for air, and slows. As soon as I catch my breath, he starts off again. We pass the fishing boats. Several men stop what they're doing to stare. At me, mostly.

We push on, veering away from the water toward the sandy bluff. As we start to climb, I realize where we're heading.

"Is it that painter?"

He looks back at me and nods, then turns and continues to climb, the back of his work shirt a triangle of sweat.

I scramble after him. It's not easy climbing a stony embankment in a formal gown. The hem is getting filthy. "But," I gasp, "what's a painter doing in a glass factory?"

He doesn't speak till we reach the grassy top. "He hasn't been able to sell his paintings. My dad got him a job in the factory. Here, we should go in."

I glance at the house—dilapidated as ever. Several people are outside, including a hard-faced man in overalls, leaning against the door. Seeing me, he pushes himself up, gives me a look that I can only think is a sneer, and walks away.

What does he have against me? *I've never* seen *him before.*

There are two others, one of them an old woman in a blue head scarf sitting cross-legged, with a wooden bowl in her lap. A younger woman, standing beside her, turns and looks at me in surprise.

I start toward her, but hesitate, seeing her unsmiling face. Finally, she nods. "Hello, Miss Tummel."

"Anna!" I seize her hand. "What are you doing here?"

"My *mamus*, she makes special *meski* for the painter." She nods at the woman, who frowns up at me.

"Your mother, yes! Hello."

No answer. Just those sharp eyes, black as gunsights.

"*Meski*," Anna explains. "It is tea. *Mamus*, she knows the plants. How you say? Herbs. Her tea make strong blood. But it is too late for the painter man."

Cole speaks up. "You mean he's *dead*?"

"He is alive. A little."

Cole takes me by the arm.

Inside, two large people crowd the dim, low-ceilinged room. When my eyes adjust, I see they are Cole's parents.

"Hello, Mrs. Havens, Mr. Havens."

Cole's mother looks me over and shakes her head. The satin ball gown doesn't help my case.

177

Cole's dad steps forward, leaning heavily on his cane, and offers a callused hand.

"I understand the painter's hurt," I say, peering about.

Havens nods. "I'll never forgive myself, getting him that job. He has no business in a glass factory. This one, especially."

"He's back there," says his wife in a flat voice.

I edge past them to the bed. A man lies in dirty work-clothes, his face smeared with ashes, eyes shut, neck and shoulder bandaged, blood seeping through the gauze.

So this is Underwood. He looks barely alive.

"I don't think you can help." Mrs. Havens has taken a seat on the other side of the bed. "Too late."

I glance from her ruddy face to his unnaturally pale one. She may be right. I can see my coming here was a last resort, after everything else failed.

"What happened?"

"Ach. That damn factory. A sheet of glass slipped and took a slice out of 'im. It would never have happened if that uncle of yours . . ."

So it's a cut, then. I can do cuts.

I kneel beside the bed for a closer look, but it's hard to concentrate with Cole's parents staring at my back. Anna has come in, too, and her mother. Just what I need, an audience.

Careful not to touch him with my glass thumb, I place my hands on the sticky gauze at the base of Underwood's neck. His blood stains my sleeve.

The pulse is weak, the pillow soaked and reeking. His eyelids flutter, mothlike, and I get the feeling—it's a feeling through my hands—that I'm losing him. There's just not enough life. I bow my head and concentrate.

My eyes are closed.

His eyes are closed.

You'd almost think we were praying.

We are.

Now my hands tingle and grow warm as I press the base of his neck more firmly. It's hard to find a pulse. For seconds, there's nothing. Then another beat.

Come on, mister.

I will my life into him. Through my hands into him.

My hands grow warmer.

Shutting my eyes tighter, I sink into myself. Not myself exactly, because I don't feel alone. We're doing this together. My life. His life. Our life.

We can do this.

No pulse. I'm counting now. Three seconds.

Five seconds!

I feel myself lose concentration. Fear does that. I glance at Cole's mother. She stares back. And there's Anna's mother. . . .

Don't look at them!

I close my eyes again. Shut out everything. Alone. Alone with this man, this Underwood. The two of us.

The one of us.

A heartbeat!

My hands grow hot.

Another heartbeat, faint as the first. Then, seconds later, another.

We stay like this for what must be minutes. The pulse is irregular, but getting stronger, the breathing more definite, as I pour my life into him. Finally, feeling woozy, I have to stop. I need to stand up, to get back some of the energy that's been drained from me; but I'm afraid to. Can he keep going on his own?

I lift my hands a few inches, but hover. His chest rises slightly, falls slightly.

I take my hands away. He keeps breathing.

I look at Cole's mother, on the other side of the bed. "What if we take off the bandage?" I ask.

She frowns. "I don't think so."

"I need to see."

She looks at me doubtfully.

"Would you do it?" I ask.

Silently, she gets up and takes my place. I'm glad she does, because a strange dizziness sweeps over me. I lean against the wall. Cole slips an arm around my shoulder. "Are you all right?"

I take a couple of slow breaths. "A little weak."

We watch as Cole's mother snips the bandages.

She gasps.

There's blood all over him. His neck, his shoulder, the mattress. But it's dried blood. *Dried blood!*

Only a narrow red line still oozes.

Cole's mother turns toward me. She starts to speak,

but can't get anything out. There are people who are criers and people who aren't. Today, she comes close. She stands, reaches for me, pulls me against her. Then pushes me roughly away, holds my shoulders, and looks at me hard.

At the sound of a moan, we turn. Underwood's head moves back and forth as if to escape a dream. I kneel beside him and hold his head to calm him.

His eyes tremble, then open.

They open wider. Bright clear blue. He's staring at me.

He tries to speak. Swallows.

Finally, in a whispery voice: *"Marina?"*

Chapter Twenty-Seven

A tear starts in the corner of his eye, a tremor in the lips, a beginning smile. "You came back," he murmurs as his eyes slowly close.

"Wait. Mr. Underwood, I'm not . . ." But I stop myself. He's asleep.

I reach for Cole's arm and struggle to my feet.

He turns to his mother. "I told you. You didn't believe me. She can do anything!"

I'm about to object when I sense someone at my elbow. It's the Gypsy woman, holding out her bowl of tea.

"*Meski,*" she says in her growly voice. "You take some."

"But it's for him."

"Yes, for him. Later. You need now."

I take the bowl, half filled with a strange-smelling brew. She nods encouragingly. "For your blood."

"My blood. Right."

I take a tentative sip, then immediately shudder and shake my head. What did she *put* in there? Out of politeness, I force myself to take another sip. Worse!

The woman takes the bowl back and looks at me. No expression. As if she's waiting. Am I supposed to say something?

But then I notice a strange feeling. I'm not quite as dizzy as before. My head's a little clearer. "Wait." I take the bowl back from her, hold it in both hands, get my courage up, and take a big swallow.

Truly horrible!

"That was good," I tell her.

She smiles, showing a gap where two teeth are missing. *"Parika tut."*

"She say tank you," Anna explains.

There are smiles around the room. The painter was dying, but now he lives!

It feels like a party, with one of the guests unconscious—the guest of honor. I kneel and examine his wound. Yes, the gash is healing, but he's dangerously weak.

No more need for bandages. There's just a shrinking red line beginning below the chin and running down to the collarbone.

"Bravo!" cries Cole's father, loudly clapping.

The noise half wakens the painter. His head moves

side to side, and he opens his eyes. Still looking foggy, he notices Cole's mother in the chair beside the bed. "You're not her."

"I'm Helen Havens," she says. "Cole's mother."

He murmurs something, and she bends in to catch it. "Where . . ." He swallows. "Where is she?"

She looks uncertain.

"I *saw* her," he says in a fierce whisper.

"Mr. Underwood, you've been hurt. I know what you think you saw, but—"

His look changes. There's suspicion in his eyes. "Why are you lying?"

"I'm not ly—"

"What have you done with her?" He strains to climb out of bed and start searching, but he can't lift his head. "She was here! *Marina!*" He must think he's shouting, but his voice is pitiful. *"Marina!"*

This is not good for him.

I step out from behind Cole. "Hello."

He subsides onto his pillow and takes a long look at me, his eyes moistening. I blush in spite of myself. No human being, certainly no man, has ever looked at me the way he's looking. "Marina," he breathes.

"It's all right. I'm here. Just rest."

He nods, submissive.

"Here, I have some medicine. It will help you." I take the bowl of lukewarm *meski* and spoon a little into his mouth. He doesn't object. I think he'd go along with anything I say. I give him another spoonful and watch him swallow.

His brow darkens. "You didn't come."

"What? When?"

"You were going to meet me, but you didn't come."

"You mean on the ship?"

He nods.

"I'm sorry. I tried. But I'm here now."

"Yes," he says. "You're here now."

"More tea?" I give him another spoonful, which he takes without complaint. "Now rest. Get your strength."

"Will you stay?"

Fear zips through me. I can't pretend forever. He'll realize I'm not Mother, and then what?

And Uncle Asa. Has he realized yet that I've gone missing?

"Of *course* I'll stay."

He sleeps a long time. Every so often, I check his pulse, and each time, it's a little steadier, a little stronger. I watch his face. It's a good face. You can tell a lot from the lines. He has worry lines, smile lines, sad lines, but nothing like the sharp verticals on Asa's face.

There's so much I want to ask him.

Anna comes up to me. "We go. *Mamus*, she leaves the *meski* for the painter. She brings more tomorrow."

I follow her outside to say goodbye and am surprised

to see it is already twilight. Her mother is there, smiling. *"Kushti bok,"* she says—goodbye—and gives my cheek a little pat with her leathery hand.

Anna hugs me briefly. I see she still has the hair clip I gave her. "You come sometime?" she says. *"Mamus* will like that."

"I want to, yes. I don't know when, but—"

"Kushti bok," she whispers.

I watch them trudge along the bluff toward the Gypsy camp till they disappear in the gloom. Below, the firth murmurs to itself. Overhead, a star blinks on. As I stand here, an unfamiliar feeling sweeps through me, making my eyes blur. It takes a moment to realize what it is.

I love these people.

Anna, Underwood, Cole, Mrs. Havens. I love them.

All the keener, then, the memory suddenly slicing through me, sickening me with shame. It's an indoor memory. You can't have such feelings out here under the sky. I was standing in Mother's bedroom, staring at her portrait, thinking: *I could hurt them.*

That can't be me. Not my thought. And yet I thought it. I remember it *thrilled* me to think it!

Who am I?

Cole comes and stands beside me. "That's an amazing thing you did," he says.

His words bring me back. I smile up at him. "I didn't know it would work. I've only done cuts and bruises."

"He was dying."

"Yes, it felt that way."

"I wonder . . . ," he says, then stops.

At that moment, Cole's mother appears at the doorway. "You should come, Cisley. He's waking up."

With dread in my stomach, I follow Cole in. *Now he's going to find out.*

Cole's dad is talking to him about the accident. Underwood only half follows him. His eyes wander around the room.

"Where is she?" says Underwood.

"Who do you mean?"

The painter closes his eyes and opens them wide, trying to focus.

"He means me, I think," I say, stepping up to the bed. "Is that right?"

"Ah," says Underwood, and sinks back.

"You're having trouble with your eyes?"

He nods. "The medicine helps some."

"The Gypsies brought it."

He seems content to be silent, but I'm not. Everything I say is a lie, and now I can't stop lying. "I like the painting you did of me," I say. "I look at it every day."

He smiles slightly. "It was easy. You were so . . ." He breaks off.

"What?"

"Happy. You had your secret." A dark thought flits across his face. "But you never told me."

What do I say to that?

"Why didn't you? I never would have left!"

Now I'm really confused.

"And then to get your letter! After all those years!"
Again, he breaks off. His eyes begin to close.

Is he going to sleep? He can't go to sleep now!

Let him rest.

No!

"After all those years *what?*"

His eyes open a slit.

"What?" I repeat.

He shakes his head. "I waited. I was there, waiting. You never came."

"The boat? In Trieste?"

"And then," he says, frowning, *"she* came."

I hold my breath. Why am I trembling?

"I knew right away," he says.

My voice is a whisper. "What did you know?"

"I never saw her before, but I knew."

"Knew . . ."

"I knew," he says, "she was *our girl.*"

Chapter Twenty-Eight

It's full dark by the time I start home. Cole offers to walk me, but I tell him I'm a big girl.

"I'll get you down to the beach. It's a tricky climb."

All right, I want to talk to him anyway.

As soon as we lower ourselves over the lip of the bluff, we're swallowed in shadow. We work our way slowly, clutching each other's arms. Finally, we reach the flat sand and the brilliance of direct moonlight.

"Thanks," I tell him. "Guess I needed your help after all."

We look at each other.

"Are you okay?" he says.

"A little stunned."

He nods. "Do you believe him?"

"Don't you?"

"He's hardly in a condition to make up lies."

I puff out a sigh. "It still hasn't hit me. My *father*. He's my *father*!"

"Strange no one ever told you."

"I know. I used to ask my mother about it when I was little. *'Where's Daddy?'* She would never give me an answer. I learned to stop asking."

Cole lays a light hand on my shoulder. "What are you going to do now?"

"I don't know. It's good your mother's staying with him. I'll come back tomorrow."

"Do you think you can?"

Good point. Asa, Janko, Strunk, and the whole blessed staff will do what they can to keep me from going anywhere.

I aim a steady look at Cole. "I will be there."

"Good," he says.

I turn and hurry off down the beach, not looking back, filled with a sense of freedom like a gust of wind blowing through me. In fact, the wind is up. It lifts the folds of my gown into shining wings, fluttering in the moonlight.

I'm all alone. No one can hear me, or save me if I need saving, and that's how I like it. Overhead, the night's on fire with stars, while down here the waves turn silver as they curve and crash, spattering me with foam. They're louder than the wind, and on a crazy impulse I roar back, a shout that's half laughter, half raw animal cry. I've never pulled a sound so loud from so deep a place. But it's a glorious night, a wild night, and

I'm wild myself. *I have a father! I have a father, and I saved his life!*

My stride turns into a skip, my skip into a dance, as the gown flows around me.

Rounding the curve of the shore, I pass the fishing boats, restless in their moorings. On the hill beyond, the castle rises. Closer now, I catch a glint on the parapet. As I suspected: it's my uncle with his field glasses, staring out. The scene strikes me as almost funny: Uncle Asa spying on me. What can he do? He's not my father. No, he is not!

I do another twirl, the gleaming gown flaring around me, and race into the water up to my knees and out again, my arms outstretched. Then I enter the hill's black shadow and start the climb.

By the time I arrive at the castle gate, I'm breathing hard. Yes, he's seen me. He knows I've escaped. And now he knows I've been in Mother's room and stolen— that's the word he'd use—stolen her gown.

I head around the side to the kitchen door and enter there. Considering how late it is, I'm not surprised the kitchen and pantry are deserted. No one hears me patter up the stairs to the second floor.

First thing to do is get to Mother's rooms, where I left my clothes. I smell my way without too much difficulty— I'm getting good at this. How silent it is in here, after my run in the wind. I feel like I'm bringing some wildness in with me, some loudness of thought that doesn't belong in this private place.

A glance in the mirror gives me a start. I knew I'd look windblown, but it's worse than I imagined! My amazing hairdo is askew, my face flushed, and the gown—I've ruined it! Look at the stains. Mud stains, bloodstains. And the hem is ripped!

"Quite an outing you had for yourself!" comes a voice.

I whirl around, my heart tumbling in my chest. *"Who's there?"*

The conch shell sits demurely on the vanity.

I let out a big breath. "You scared me!"

The shell makes no comment. Not one for small talk.

"What am I going to do about this gown?" I ask.

"What do you mean? You're going to hang it up where you found it."

"But it's a wreck!"

"Well, it wasn't made for crawling in the dirt."

"Thanks. I know that."

"Just do as I say."

"Hang it up? Isn't there someone I should give it to? There's a woman in town. . . ."

Silence.

"All right, then." I pull the gown off over my head and go to the closet—that amazing closet—and hang it on its hanger. Turning to leave, I notice a tiny point of light floating past. Then another. More tiny lights sail by. The closet is growing brighter! I stare at the gown, now swarming with lights, like a thousand golden bees! It reminds me of my mother's magic tricks.

"Mother?" I listen. "Mother, are you here?"

No sound but the vague whisperings of a thousand lights nibbling and mending. Soon there are fewer of them. Another minute and the last one blinks away, leaving the shimmering gown, a sheath of pale blue satin, perfect as the first moment I saw it.

I back out, unable to take my eyes off it.

"Did *you* do that?" I ask the shell.

No answer.

I climb into my own clothes—plain dress, floppy bow—hopelessly childish. I've got to stop letting Miss Porlock pick my clothes.

With the shell under my arm, I head down the corridor and into the Mirror Maze. The pattern has changed since this afternoon, but I understand the principle of the thing and, after a few false starts, get through.

Before long, I'm at my own door.

Uh-oh. The person I least want to see.

"Where have you been?" Uncle Asa demands, getting up from the sofa. He looks pale.

"I—"

"Never mind. Something has happened."

"The black rose! You did it?"

"No. Nothing to do with that."

He's having a hard time saying what it is. At least it doesn't seem to be about me.

"Is it that terrible?" I say.

"Did I say it was terrible?"

His face tells me it's pretty terrible.

He stares at me grimly. "I was on the roof tonight. I saw her."

"You saw—"

"I saw your mother! *She's back!*"

Chapter Twenty-Nine

First thing in the morning, Janko appears and takes me to the laboratory. Asa doesn't look up as I come in, so I just stand there. Finally, I can't help myself: "You're sure it was Mother?"

He glances at me, quick and sharp, then goes back to packing fertilizer around the base of a dying rose. "Of course I'm sure. It was her gown. The way she moves. Everything."

I step closer. "But where is she now?"

He stops puttering, leans against the workbench. "That's what bothers me."

"Not in her rooms?"

"We looked. The lock was broken into. It must have been her. She didn't have a key, obviously."

"No, I guess she wouldn't have."

"I had the whole staff searching. Didn't you hear them bumping around?"

I don't say anything more. Why don't I? Why don't I tell him the truth?

My silence is a lie. Am I afraid of his anger? Yes. But something else. I'm like the prisoner who's found a sharp object in her cell. It may be useless, but until I know more, I'll keep it in my pocket. My quiet lie.

I *have* to get out of the castle. I've got to see Peter Underwood (still can't say the word *father*), but I'm stuck. In fact, for the next six hours, I'm forced to help Asa with his failing experiments. He's quiet, answering questions with grunts, asking for tools by pointing. Still rattled by last night.

Rattled, not happy. *His sister returns from the dead, and he's not happy about it.*

Asa takes off his gloves and drops them on the table. "It's not working," he says, frowning at the latest grafting experiment. "There's something we're missing."

I could have told him that weeks ago.

"There's another test I want to try, but we can't do it today. Here, help me with this." He has me wash out the tubes and replant one of the rosebushes at the end of the table. After that, I can go. Not where I want to. I can go to my chemistry lesson with Miss Porlock.

I find her in my sitting room, poring over her Latin dictionary. She closes it quickly and lays it on top of another book, a fat, leather-bound thing with a split spine. "Hello, dear!" she says brightly. "You're finished early!"

"Uncle Asa let me go. What are you reading?"

"Just something your uncle asked me to translate. His Latin isn't very good."

"Let me see."

"My dear, I'm afraid your Latin isn't up to it, either."

"It's that book, isn't it? The one that Strunk brought up. Uncle Asa said he hadn't ordered it." I pick it up and finger the Gothic lettering, the gold leaf mostly gone. "What does the title mean?"

"*Compendium Magisterium*? Just what it sounds like, a magisterial compendium."

"Miss Porlock."

"It's a collection of instructions on various subjects."

"Anything on black roses?"

I detect a flinch before she answers. "That's the part your uncle wants me to translate."

I hand it back. "So translate it for me."

"Cisley, really. That chapter is twenty pages long. I've just started."

I take one of her ginger cookies and snap it in my teeth.

"Anyway," she says, sipping her chamomile, "we have more important things to talk about, don't we? The periodic table?"

Count on her not to forget.

After Miss Porlock has tortured me sufficiently with

the elements of helium, argon, and radon, she gathers her books and heads to her room, leaving the ginger cookies to tide me over till dinner. Wish I had Elwyn to feed them to.

I open the door and listen as the last tour group of the day shuffles past. Is this my chance? I'm in my usual clothes, so I wouldn't draw attention from people who think they're seeing my mother. I look down the corridor, then hurry and join the crowd as they start down the staircase. Still no sign of my keepers, just that tour guide up front giving the history of the chandeliers.

I'm nearly to the bottom before I spot Strunk, arms folded, staring up at me. One of his white-fringed eyebrows twitches.

"Hi, Mr. Strunk."

He speaks not a word, merely points a pudgy finger upward.

"I was just going to the kitchen. Mrs. Quay is saving me some scones."

"You need to be upstairs. I will alert Mrs. Quay about the scones."

"Thank you, Mr. Strunk."

Slink. Slank. Slunk. Up to my room again.

Twenty minutes later, dinner arrives under a silver cloche. No scones. I nibble my nut-encrusted flounder and stare out over the darkening firth. Night coming, and I still haven't figured a way to get out of here.

"Why don't we take a stroll down to your mother's rooms?"

I whirl around. There sits the conch on the night-stand.

"Now?"

"When better?"

I take another bite of roast potato and slip a warm roll in my pocket. One of the footmen, I notice as I step out, has been stationed by the top of the staircase. That's new. Don't tell me they don't trust me!

I give him a wave and head to the right. An innocent stroll. The maze offers fewer challenges to me these days, now that I understand the principle. It's just irritating that I have to deal with it at all. I'm soon in front of Mother's door.

"Why don't we do your hair again?" says the shell.

"Really? Why?"

No answer.

I sit at the vanity. Playing dress-up is fine, but I've got places to go. Still, when the last comb is in place, I can't help marveling. *Is this really Cisley Thummel?*

"Yes, it is," the voice says.

I hold the shell up. "How did you do that? You read my mind!"

"Did I? Maybe you read your own?"

That stops me.

What's in my mind? My own thoughts? Someone else's? When I'm in this room, I hardly know. I decide to do a test. "So," I say, "tell me what I'm thinking now."

Silence.

"Really, tell me. I want to know if you can read my mind."

"You're thinking about that book."

That's right! I'm thinking about that fat old Latin book Miss Porlock's so secretive about. "That's amazing!"

"Not really. You know we don't need words."

I take that in. It's true; this is no ordinary talking shell. "I bet," I say, "you even know what's *in* the book."

"Only the good parts."

"The parts about the rose."

No reply.

A thought suddenly strikes me. "You *sent* that book, didn't you?"

"Now, how could I do that?"

"I don't know, but you did."

"I may have whispered a word to a receptive ear."

"What receptive ear?"

"Don't bother your head. Let's take a peek at that gown again. See how it looks on you."

I give the shell my hardest stare and speak into the point of the spiral. "I know you have a reason for this. Do you mind telling me what it is?"

"You need a passport. A way to go in and out without your uncle's seeing you."

"Won't he see me?"

"He will see your *mother.*"

"Ah."

"Now go."

I don't question. Anyway, I love that soft waterfall of satin. I run to get it. As before, it forms itself perfectly to my body—tucks, buttons, and clasps. I feel *electric*.

"Now," says the shell, "you're ready to go visiting."

"But how?"

"The same way he came to visit your mother."

My eyes widen. *Underwood visited Mother? Here?* "Show me!"

"You've never been all the way to the back of the closet, have you?"

"No," I say, "I haven't." I leap up, grab my talkative friend, and run into the closet. Dimly lit gowns whisper among themselves, passing secrets. *Are they talking about me?* I venture on, no end in sight. An infinite aisle of dresses stretches ahead.

I notice a movement in the distance. It's someone hurrying toward me! She comes closer, slows as I slow. The aisle narrows to a mirror. The closet does end after all. It ends with me.

"It doesn't really, you know," says a voice close by.

I look at the shell. There it goes again, reading my thoughts. "It doesn't?"

"Touch your heart."

A strange request, but I've learned to listen when the shell tells me something. I place my hand over my heart.

"No." The tone is impatient. "Touch your heart in the *mirror*."

I gaze at my reflection, at this strangely glamorous self, half me, half Marina, and reach out and touch its heart.

The mirror slides aside.

The way ahead is dimmer, almost dark, but this is no time to hesitate. I follow the continuing corridor. Dusty, empty, no clothes brushing against me. I'm not sure about this world behind the mirror.

Soon the floor begins to tilt downward, slightly at first, then more steeply. I have trouble standing and can barely see where I'm going.

A muffled voice.

"What did you say?"

"I said, sit down or fall down."

I sit.

The floor here is waxed to a high polish and curves in a spiral. I start sliding. What little light remains shows me a narrow staircase to my left, hugging the circular wall. Then all light is gone, the tilt gets steeper, and for seconds I careen through darkness, finally bumping to a cushioned stop. My heart beats madly as I look from nothing to nothing.

Slowly, my eyes adjust. A thin right angle of light tells me a door's in front of me.

"Everybody out," says the shell.

A little wobbly, I get to my feet and push open the narrow door to a gust of salt air and the pounce of waves. The moonlit beach stretches below me.

"Wonderful!"

"Have a nice visit."

"Aren't you coming?"

"Leave me here, inside the door. That's it."

"Are you sure?"

"It's not safe out there for breakables. I'll be here when you get back."

"All right."

Moments later, shoes in hand, I race barefoot along the wet sand toward the cabin of Peter Underwood.

Chapter Thirty

"There! See her? She's come back!"

"That ain't her."

"It's a ghost, like they said."

"What's wrong with you? It's the daughter! Can't you see?"

A knot of workers pauses below the bluff to watch me coming. The night shift, I'm guessing, on their way to the glass factory, and they don't look pleased to see a fancy young lady in a ball gown skipping about on the beach.

"You're right," says one as I pass. "It's the crazy daughter."

"Hi, everybody!" I call. No one answers.

They don't know how keen my sense of smell is.

Ground-in grime, scorch marks, and chemical stink ride the light breeze.

That and something else: the smell of resentment.

I start the climb to the painter's cabin. The workers are almost invisible now, diminished in darkness. Except for the gleam of moonlight glancing off their caps, you'd think they didn't exist.

To Uncle Asa, they don't.

I'm breathing hard by the time I reach the top. No one in sight. A dim glow from the window is the only sign anyone's here. There's a man in there who believes he's my father. He also believes I'm my own mother.

I knock on the door. No answer. Knock a little louder. Nothing.

I push the door two creaks and step in. A kerosene lamp by the bed haloes the painter and Cole's mother. Underwood is propped in sitting position, but his head is back and his eyes closed.

Mrs. Havens slumps in her chair, snoring.

I smile to think this could be a painting by Underwood, the celebrated artist.

Don't wake them.

Most of the cabin is dim to dark, but I see well enough to look through the paintings against the wall. There are dozens. Strong, confident work, I can see that. There's the one of me on the seawall with Elwyn. The more I look at it, the better I like it. The painter gave me a look I wish I had—the visionary peering into the distance, or the future, or something. *Visionary with Lobster*, he could call it.

Imagine what it must have meant to him, seeing the girl he thinks is his daughter—to want to paint her, capture her, but not approach.

Why didn't he just come up to me? I wouldn't have bitten him.

Elwyn might have.

He stayed away, but close.

Mrs. Havens's snore becomes a snort that wakes her up. She rubs her eyes roughly and squints them open. "Oh Jesus, Mary!" she cries, seeing me.

"Hello, Mrs. Havens."

"I thought you was a ghost!"

"You're not the only one. Some men down on the beach thought I was Mother."

"Likely, in that outfit."

"I don't think they cared for me."

She grunts.

"What?"

"I'm still working on liking you myself." She adjusts her shawl around her shoulders. "You come to see the patient, I expect."

I look over at Underwood.

"Whatever that awful mess the Gypsies brought him," she says, "it's bucked him up pretty good. I wouldn't go near it, myself."

"I don't blame you."

"He's starting to mind it. It's how I know he's better."

As if he knows we're talking about him, Underwood fidgets and opens his eyes. He looks confused, but then sees me. "You're back!"

"No," I say quickly, "it's not me. I mean . . ."

He cocks his head.

"I mean, I'm not Mother."

Come on, Cisley, you can make sense if you try.

I glance over at Mrs. Havens.

"Mr. Underwood," I say, "do I look like Marina?"

He looks closer. Closer still.

"You really don't recognize me?"

I know you've only seen me from a distance, and dressed differently, but . . .

"You painted me. With the lobster?"

His eyes widen and clear. He sits up straighter. For seconds, he says nothing, just takes me in.

Say something. Why doesn't he say something?

"Is it possible?" he whispers.

I nod vigorously. "I'm Cisley."

A quick sunrise of pleasure. "Marina's daughter!"

I swallow hard. "And . . . *yours*?"

His eyes suddenly brim. Then mine do, too. I take a step toward him. He raises his arms. I fall into them.

"My girl," he murmurs. "My little girl."

Warm tears drop on my neck.

My throat tightens off speech. What would I say anyway? *Father? Dad?* I've never spoken such words in my life.

What do I do with a father?

I pull away and look at this man, this father. His lined face glistens from the edges of his eyes to the slightly trembling corners of his mouth.

God knows what my own face looks like, streaked with tears and makeup.

"You're so beautiful," he says.

That actually makes me laugh. "Must be the dress."

"Marina's?"

I nod, still gulping tears. "A long story."

He lays a quiet hand on mine. "I think we both have long stories to tell."

Chapter Thirty-One

On my way out, I practically knock into Cole, just coming in. He looks at me oddly. Must be the hair. I keep forgetting what's on top of my head.

Finally, I manage a "Hi!"

He sweeps his own out-of-control hair back from his face. "I didn't know you were here."

"Actually, I'm going."

"Oh."

"Well," I say brightly, "I've got to get some things, don't I? I can't very well go around wearing a ball gown all the time!"

"What!"

I break out in a crazy grin. "I'm going to live here!"

Cole is struck silent.

"Why shouldn't I? He's my father!"

He waits for me to go on. That's what I like about him. He lets a person take her time. I glance in Underwood's direction. "We've been talking. It's really true!"

"You're sure?"

"Yes, yes! It all makes sense. There's a lot I don't know yet, but yes."

"That you, Cole?" Mrs. Havens's voice, trying to be quiet.

Cole and I head to the back. I see that Mr. Underwood—I mean my father—has drifted to sleep. All that talking must have worn him out.

"You doing okay, Mom?" says Cole quietly.

"Terrible, but I can last until you walk Cisley home."

I start to object, but she holds up a hand. "It's almost midnight. No time for a girl to be wandering by herself."

Cole looks at me. "Cis says she's going to live here."

"So she says. I don't think she's actually thought it out."

"What's there to think about?" I huff.

"For one thing, dear, there's nowhere to turn around. The place is hardly big enough for one."

"I don't need to turn around!"

Mrs. Havens looks down, but I can see she's smiling. That makes me mad. "I don't *care* where I sleep. I'll sleep outside!"

"With the sand crabs," she supplies.

Infuriating woman!

"She's right."

I swivel around. It's my father, looking at me with a comfortable smile.

I kneel and take his hand. "You're awake."

"I'm glad you want to stay."

"Oh, I do!"

"But Mrs. Havens is right. The place isn't ready for you."

He must see my expression. Hard to miss.

"But we'll get it ready. Meantime, would you visit me?"

I sigh. "Of course. Every chance."

"And could you . . . ?"

"What? Anything."

"Could you ask your mother to come? Even a short visit." Again my face betrays me, because he hurries on. "I know she wouldn't want to stay. She's a very grand woman."

He doesn't know.

"Father?"

"She needs her servants and . . ." He twirls his hand. "All the rest."

"Father." I pause, gathering my courage. "I don't know where she is. I'm trying to find out."

Fear widens his eyes. "She's missing?"

"Since Trieste."

"That was months ago!"

"I know."

"This is terrible!" He closes his eyes, remembering.

"At first, I thought she'd changed her mind. Then I saw you, so I was sure she was coming. But she didn't!" He looks at me helplessly. "I thought it must be part of her plan, and that she'd meet me later. She's so strong, so clever. Nothing can stop her from doing what she wants."

"Well, something did."

"Here I've been feeling sorry for myself."

"Don't worry. I'll find her. I'll find her and bring her here." I pat his hand and stand up. "You just get better." I glance at Cole. "Looks like I'll have to stay in the castle a while longer. I wouldn't find any clues out here."

He nods. "I'll walk you."

"I'll be fine."

"You walk her, Cole," says Mrs. Havens.

I try to argue, but he steers me out the door. It occurs to me that maybe I shouldn't object so much.

We're at the edge of the bluff, about to descend. It's clouding up, but just now there's a break, and the moon blazes so brightly that we pause.

"So," he says, "you found your father."

"It's tremendous. He didn't know I existed till a year ago, when he saw an article somewhere that talked about Marina Thummel and her daughter—me! He had to find out how old this daughter was. When he learned I was twelve, he felt sure."

"And he's followed you around ever since?"

"Followed her. He says he tried everything to get her

212

back. Even sent her a white rose every day, no matter where she was. He was doing it right up till his accident."

Cole looks thoughtful. "Why did they break up?"

"I don't know. He says she wouldn't speak to him for years. Until Trieste."

"What happened there, I wonder?"

"He didn't say, but she finally agreed to go away with him. With me."

We start down, lowering ourselves over the lip of the bluff into shadow, holding each other's hands to keep balance. We can't see a thing, our feet feeling for solid ground. I think I'm doing pretty well until my ankle twists on a loose stone. The next moment, my arms flail, pulling Cole off balance. He barely catches himself. "Easy now," he says, steadying me.

"Thanks," I say to the darkness.

We make it to the bottom.

"You okay?" he says.

I nod. "You?"

We're standing at the exact dividing line between shadow and moonlight. Half his face is visible.

I like what I see.

His warm hand feels good in mine.

I should let go of it.

Just slightly, he squeezes my hand.

Did I really feel that? His grip tightens a little more. I'm not holding his hand. He's holding mine.

I look into his face. Half of it.

It bends toward me, and I lift my face to meet it, my shadow joining his.

"Hey, hey!" Laughter and loud clapping. Shocked, I spin around to see a tall boy step from the shadows. He's followed by two other boys, younger.

Cole looks a little stunned, but recovers. "Nicolae," he says.

Now I recognize him. Anna's brother. The others I'd seen in the Gypsy camp.

"Not interrupting?" Nicolae says.

Cole doesn't answer.

"Good idea," Nicolae goes on. "Kiss her. Maybe she gets you a job."

"What are you talking about?"

"The uncle fires us today. All the Roma people."

My thumb is clicking madly. "Oh no!" I say.

He ignores me, just talks to Cole. "He wants we should go. No more dirty Gypsies in his nice town."

I'm bursting to speak, to tell him that I'll talk to Asa. I'll make him change his mind. But the scorn on Nicolae's face stops me. I am the spoiled rich girl.

"That's bad," says Cole.

"Yes, you are sorry. I am sure your girlfriend, she is sorry, too."

"It's not her fault."

"No. Of course. But since she comes to our camp, things go badly for us. He doesn't like that we talk to her."

"So," says Cole, "you think he's punishing you?"

"Let *me* talk to Asa," I burst out. "He can't do this!"

Nicolae ignores me. "Go," he says, with a flip of his hand. "Do what you are doing. But remember: a castle of glass can be broken."

He strides into the shadows with his silent friends. Cole and I watch them disappear. We are no longer holding hands.

"I'd better go," I say quietly.

"I'll walk you."

"No. I'll be fine."

"Cisley, there are angry people out here. It's not just the Gypsies. The factory isn't safe to work in, and your uncle doesn't seem to care. After my dad got hurt last year—"

"Your father?"

"His foot was crushed. He's had to use a cane ever since."

"No wonder your mother doesn't like me."

"She's coming around. Anyway," he says, "you shouldn't be walking home by yourself."

"I have to. Why do you think I'm wearing these silly clothes?"

"I thought you liked dressing up."

"To go climbing around on sand dunes? No, it's to fool my uncle. He's always spying on me. From a distance, he thinks I'm Mother. As far as he knows, I'm still in my room."

"Smart."

"Wasn't my idea. A friend suggested it."

"What friend?"

"Don't be jealous." I throw him a smile. "Or do." With that, I give him a little wave and start down the beach. But then I look back. There are thirty feet of wind between us, just like the first time I saw him, up on the seawall. "Hey, Cole!" I call.

"What?" he shouts back.

"Take care of my father!"

"I will!"

I continue on, my torn hem trailing in foam from retreating waves. The wind plays with my hair and flutters through the folds of the gown. It's been an amazing night. I talked with my father! And there was that moment with Cole. That almost moment.

Why am I depressed?

Rounding the curve of the shoreline, I know very well why. Up on the far cliff, the Crystal Castle glitters, a glass spike driven into the heart of the town.

I don't want to go there. I don't want to endure the stink of Asa's laboratory to help him create an impossible flower. The idea of it feels evil to me, like a velvet death. How much I prefer my father's white roses, sent each day to an empty room. Still, somewhere in that strange castle, there's a clue to my mother. There's bound to be!

Coming closer, I can just make out the secret entrance, above the seawall. You'd never know it was there. I clamber up, my gown catching on the rocks. The clouds are thickening, the moon ducking in and out. Little white-caps form in the firth. There'll be rain by morning.

"Okay, old friend," I say, pulling open the door and peering in. "What have you been up to all this time?"

No answer.

The moon, briefly free of cloud, sends a shaft through the entrance, alighting on several small objects. I look closer. Stoop. Pick up one of them.

Bits of something hard.

My shell! My beautiful shell has been smashed to pieces!

Chapter Thirty-Two

It was just a shell. Why am I crying?

It was more than that. It was a *voice*!

Picking up every fragment I can find, even the smallest, I start up the narrow staircase. After a few steps, the darkness becomes absolute, and I hug the curving wall. A fall here would be serious.

Who did this? Who would break my shell?

How did they know where it was?

Dim light from above begins to reach me. I can make out the stairs, arched beams, and part of the chute I slid down during my earlier escape. Halfway, I pause, the shell pieces digging into my hand. I'm so disheartened I can hardly go on.

Finally, I reach the top and step past the mirror into the familiar world of Mother's closet, with its swaying array. The gowns used to feel so friendly as I swept past them. Now I don't know. I don't know anything.

There's the silver hanger. Yes, why not? I slip off the gown and hang it up, then watch as tiny lights begin circling it. More and more lights, brighter and brighter, till the gown is dazzling. I leave them to their work and continue out to the bedroom.

Sitting at the vanity, I set the fragments in front of me. "I'm sorry," I whisper. "I should have taken you with me."

Slowly, I start the job of taking down my hair and brushing it out. It's quite a tangle. Three times the tangle, in the three-way mirror.

I pause midstroke. The light hairs on my arm begin to rise. *Someone else is in the room! I'm sure of it!* I stare into the mirror, trying to see behind me; but there's nothing, just candlelit dimness.

So why is my breath frozen in my chest?

Slowly, I turn.

No one.

I peer into shadowy corners, even under the bed. Then I go to the closet and trot all the way down and back among the glowing gowns. I must be crazy. But when I sit at the vanity again, the feeling is stronger than ever.

Just concentrate on what you're doing.

I move one side of the three-paneled mirror a couple of inches to see myself better, and now, instead of three Cisleys, there are six, reflections within reflections. I'm not sure, in my present mood, that I want to see that many Cisleys.

It's interesting, though. I move the other side an inch or so. Suddenly, there's an endless line of Cisleys, every one of them with tangled hair.

All but one.

Again, that freezing in my chest. One of the reflections, far down the line, is *not me*!

"Mother!" I cry aloud.

There's no doubt. It's my mother's face, behind a dozen of my own, staring wildly out at me, her mouth wide.

"Mother! Is it you?"

Her mouth forms the word *"Help!"* Even with no sound, I can see it.

"How can I help you? Where *are* you?"

She keeps mouthing the same *"Help! Help!"*

A noise behind me makes me turn. A soft, jangling sound, of someone fiddling with keys. My heart jumps as I hear the door fly open.

A familiar voice from the outer room: "Somebody has to fix that lock."

"Miss Porlock!"

Miss P. looks into the bedroom. "Cisley! There you are!" *Of all the times for her to interrupt . . .*

"I've come to warn you!" She stops herself, frowns, her forehead shining. "You're naked!"

"I am not naked!" True, I'm in my underthings, but you could hardly say . . .

"Why are you naked? And your hair!"

"I'll explain all that. Warn me about what?"

"Oh!" Miss P. collapses in a velvet chair, looking faint. "I've been translating Latin."

"What?" I can't believe this.

"The book," she gasps out. "The book your uncle gave me."

"I remember."

Casually, I move one side of the mirror a couple of inches. Mother disappears.

"Please get some clothing on, Cisley! What do you mean, going about like that?"

"What about the book?"

"The book. It tells in very considerable detail how to create a black rose."

"Good."

She lays a hand on her bosom. *"Not* good. It talks about 'golden blood.'"

I wait. Why does it always take so long to get to the point?

"That's what it calls a magician's blood. I don't suppose it's actually golden. Probably just a figure of speech."

"What *about* it?"

"Don't you see? He needs the blood to make the rose. That's *you*, Cisley. You're the one with the magic. He wants your blood!"

She sees the doubting look on my face.

"Listen to me. Your life's in danger!"

"I don't think so. Uncle Asa is not a nice man, but I really doubt that he'd kill me."

"Can you be sure? You know how obsessed he is."

"But I'm his niece!"

"How much do you suppose that counts with him? If I recall, he already hit you once." She struggles to her feet, holding on to the chair back. "This whole business about black roses, I don't like it. I've never liked it."

"Well, don't give him the book. Say you lost it."

"Too late. He snatched the translation away before I was even finished. If I were you, I'd hide."

"I will not hide. I'm sure you're wrong about my uncle." *Well*, I think, *I'm almost sure.*

"Oh, Cisley." She looks at me sadly. "You know so little about life. You've grown up without a father, and practically without a mother. . . ."

"That's not true."

"I wish it weren't, dear. Be honest. How much of a mother has Marina been to you?"

My cheeks flush. To say such a thing in this room! "She's been . . ." I falter only a moment. ". . . a fine mother!"

"Yes, well, you have to believe that, I suppose." Miss P. pats my shoulder. "Anyway, you can believe in *me*. I'll protect you with my last breath. Your uncle will not lay a finger on you."

"Thank you, Miss P."

"Not a finger! Now," she adds, turning to the door, "do put some clothes on, for heaven's sake."

As she leaves, I quickly readjust the mirror until it again shows a long line of reflections, Cisley upon Cisley. There! Toward the end: Mother.

I flinch.

I've never seen such fury on a human face.

Chapter Thirty-Three

"Have you *seen* her? I know she's here somewhere. Even the tourists have seen her!" Uncle Asa's shouting because of the rain roaring down on the glass roof of the laboratory. Maybe he'd be shouting anyway. He lurches around, clearing off the worktable, pushing pots of roses to the side.

I'm looking out at the rain so I don't have to watch him. I can't see much. It's been evening all day.

"I've had the place searched, top to bottom. I'm going crazy!"

I glance down. He went past crazy a long time ago. I could so easily calm his mind, if I'd just admit that I was the one he saw on the beach. But I won't do that. I need to be able to come and go.

Why hasn't he said anything about the experiment

he's preparing? The one Miss Porlock thinks he'd kill for?

The rain pelts down harder. Shadows of streaming water slide along the glass walls and down Asa's face like sheets of tears. He's gotten older in the months since he started these experiments. I notice for the first time the small hard lines that have settled around the corners of his mouth.

He drags a tub of topsoil from under the counter. All the old soil has been thrown out. He wants to start fresh.

There on the table is that Latin book, with its stiff vellum pages. Several sheets of paper stick out of it. Miss P.'s translation?

He stops tugging at the tub. "I never believed such things," he says.

I'm not sure I heard, with all the rain. "What?"

"I said, I never used to believe in such things. I always thought there was a trick, because there always was. But I see it's true. It really *is* possible for the dead to haunt us."

Our eyes meet. The rain continues its drumroll. "So," I say, raising my voice to be heard, "you think she's dead?"

"Don't you?"

Somber thought. I saw her in the vanity mirror last night, but what did I see? Was it Mother, or was it the ghost of Mother? Maybe Asa isn't the only one being haunted.

He thumps a sealed carton on the workbench and

slits it open. New instruments—vials, electric wires, test tubes.

"Don't we have these already?" I venture.

"I'm getting rid of everything I failed with."

Then you should start with me. "Sounds like an important experiment."

He holds up one of the new test tubes, then another.

I hear a ticking sound and realize I'm tapping the glass tip of my thumb. "Sounds like you think this might work," I say, louder.

He grunts, sets the test tubes on a rack.

"Can you *tell* me about it?"

He looks over as if just remembering I'm here. "You'll find out tomorrow."

He's avoiding me. Won't even look at me. "Can't you tell me *now*?"

"No, I cannot. Too complicated."

Click-click.

"Because," I say, pausing for courage, "I don't think I'll be helping you with this one."

"What!" He glares at me. "What do you *mean*? You're essential. The experiment can't be done without you."

"Why can't it?"

His lips tighten. The lines at the corners of his mouth harden. "Will you stop *interrogating* me?"

"I want to know why it can't be done without me."

"You're a very irritating young woman, do you know that?"

"Tell me!"

He rubs his face with both hands, as if to erase me from his mind. "If you must know, you have something I need."

Click-click, click-click, click-click.

"A special ingredient," he adds.

Worse and worse.

"*What* ingredient?"

"Now, that's enough! We'll go over all this tomorrow!"

"I'm not coming! You can't make me!"

Uncle Asa looks at me strangely. "What's gotten into you? I very well *can* make you."

"No, you can't! You're not my father!"

"Well, that's one thing to be grateful for anyway." He gestures to the supply cabinet. "I want you to take those old instruments and put them in the trash, then wipe down the shelves. After that—"

"No."

"No?"

Instead of answering, I stalk over to the door and yank it open. The rain pounds down outside. I turn. "I found him, you know."

He cocks his head as if to hear me correctly.

"My father!" I'm practically shouting. "I *found* him. I'm going to *live* with him. You can't stop me."

Asa stares at me. "You mean that Underwood creature?"

"He's a better person than you are."

"Does he want more money?"

"Does he what?"

"Does he want *more money*?"

I'd been feeling triumphant up to that moment.

He jumps into the gap. "Tell him it's too late. She's *gone*."

"What are you talk—"

"He didn't tell you? He wouldn't. Might jeopardize his chances."

Now I'm bewildered.

"I paid him to go away," Asa explains. "And go away he did, like a good dog."

"You *paid* him? Why?"

"It was a test. He failed. And now, it seems, he's back for more. Well, you can tell him—"

Whatever he wants me to tell him I don't hear, because I've gone outside and slammed the door. There's Janko, in a slouch hat and slicker, standing under the canopy, smoking. He eyes me curiously, but doesn't move to stop me as I march past into the wind-driven rain.

I'm down in my room, dripping. Asa says my father abandoned Mother. He's lying, of course. Isn't he? He'd say anything to keep me here, now that he needs . . .

That's what it's about. The so-called golden blood. He wouldn't tell me what he's planning. Why wouldn't he, unless it's something horrible?

I was going to stay and search for clues to Mother, but Miss Porlock is right. I've got to get out of here.

I change quickly into dry things and hunt around for a

suitcase. There isn't one. My eyes light on the silk pillowcase. With trembling hands, I lay out the essentials—underwear, hairbrush, a second skirt and blouse—then load them into the pillowcase and tie the opening.

Wait. I pick up Cole's little wooden turtle and slip it in my pocket. I'll need it for luck.

I'll also need my hooded cape against the rain. Draping it over my arm, I hoist my bundle and peer out. Strunk's echoey voice reaches me from downstairs, talking to Mrs. Quay. Can't go that way. I head to the right, toward the maze and Mother's rooms beyond. The way is different this time, with subtler illusions, deceptive doors. Uncle Asa, it seems, is more determined than ever to keep me from getting away; but he has forgotten my sense of smell. I bang my head against a glass partition and nearly step in a hole, but the scent of the white rose guides me through.

About to step out of the maze, I hear a male voice just ahead. A woman laughs in reply. The man lowers his voice confidentially. The woman giggles. I know them. It's that new young valet with one of the housemaids, Bonnie, the very one I bribed to deliver a message to Cole.

How do I get past them?

Here I am, weighed down with my bulging pillowcase, and I can't go forward because a servant is chatting up his girlfriend!

Not a finger. Yes, I remember. *Your uncle will not lay a finger on you.*

Miss Porlock.

I've been to her rooms only a few times, but I remember the way. Hitching the pillowcase on my shoulder, I retrace my steps, silently cursing Asa's obstacles, then hurry past my rooms and on around the curve of the corridor to a dead end.

In the middle of the dead end stands a door.

I raise my hand. Lower it. Take a deep breath.

I knock.

Chapter Thirty-Four

"Go away!" A voice like an angry crow.

"Miss Porlock, it's me!"

Silence.

I'm about to knock again when I hear a metallic slap, and a peephole slides open. A large eye fills the space. "Cisley?"

"Let me in, please."

The peephole closes. After a pause, I hear the snap of a lock, followed by a scrape and a loud click. The door sighs inward.

"Cisley! What are you—"

"Can we talk inside?" I practically push past her. "I don't want anyone to see me."

She lets me by and closes the door, resetting the locks and sliding the bolt in place.

"That's a lot of locks."

"You can't be too careful," she says. "Spies every-where."

"Really? Spies?"

"They call them servants. But they all report to Mr. Strunk, who reports to your uncle. Never mind. You're here now."

I peer through the gloom. The air is heavy with the smells of old face powder and tired perfume, mixed with a hint of lamp oil. Not at all like my bright, airy apart-ment overlooking the Firth of Before.

"Are you running away?" she says, noticing my bun-dle. "Why didn't you say so?" She leads me to the sit-ting room, which is scarcely brighter than the entrance. There's a window, but thick draperies block whatever light might find its way around this side of the castle.

"Let's get a better look at you." She lights a lamp and sets the shade over it. "Now then," she says, "tell Miss Porlock what happened."

I slump into an overstuffed armchair and immedi-ately sneeze. Doesn't anyone dust this place? "Well," I say, "I realized you were right."

Miss P. sits on the edge of the adjoining sofa. In the lamplight, the knob of her forehead glows like a lump of gold. "About the blood?"

I nod.

"So you're running away. I think that's wise, but why come to me?"

"I thought maybe . . ."

"I could hide you?"

Another nod.

Slowly, she rubs her shiny forehead, as if to help her think. "That it should come to this," she mutters. "Afraid for your life in your own house."

"It would be just for a little while, until—"

She reaches out and catches my wrist. Turns my hand over. "Cisley! Oh my dear! What *happened*?"

Under the lamp, the glass thumb shines.

I blush, as though I'm guilty of something. Guilty, at least, of hiding it from her for weeks.

"This is *not* a cut," she says.

"I know."

"Cisley?"

"It came from the mirror Mother used in her magic trick."

"The *black* mirror? Oh no!" Miss P. launches herself to her feet and stalks about, muttering, her whole body agitated. I make out the word *horrible!* repeated under her breath.

"It's nobody's fault, Miss P. I was careless, that's all."

"Between your mother and your uncle, it's a wonder you've survived this long."

"But I'm telling you, I did this myself."

"Yes. And no one was watching out for you, making sure you were safe. Just *selfish*, both of them!"

She isn't being fair. Mother disappeared long before

my accident with the mirror. It *is* nice, though, to see someone angry on my account. Who else in this place even cares about me?

"Can I stay here tonight?"

"You must!" Her anger melts to motherliness. "You saw all the locks I have. No one will bother us."

I believe her. For the first time in hours, I begin to relax.

It turns out Miss P. has a tiny kitchen, hardly big enough for a person with her bone structure, but with room to make tea, which she does and which I don't mind as much as I usually do. She shows me around her cushion-stuffed rooms, stopping to gaze up at a large painting.

"Who's that?" I'm staring at a regal woman reclining on a couch, while two children, boy and girl, play a board game on the carpet. Another girl, larger, sits off on her own, with a knitting basket on her lap. A small dog pokes its head from under the couch.

"You don't recognize them?"

I look closer. Shake my head.

"That's Grandma Isabel and the children—surely you recognize your mother and Asa?"

That boy in short pants playing on the floor? Did he really turn into the Amazing Thummel, Illusionist? Was he nasty even then?

And Mother! Ten or eleven years old. Already so pretty! Curls and flashing eyes.

"And the other girl?"

"That's me."

"Really!" I squint. "Hard to see her face."

"Isn't it." Miss Porlock's lips compress. "The artist felt my face would not add to the beauty of the composition, so he put me in shadow."

"That's terrible!"

"I suppose I'm lucky to be in the picture at all."

"But you're related. Aren't you? Sort of?"

"I'm their half sister."

I stare at her. I'd always thought she was some sort of cousin, twice removed. But she's my *aunt*! "You're really Mother's half sister?"

"The wrong half, apparently."

"I don't understand."

"My mother had the bad taste to have an affair with the gardener, a fellow named Porlock. No education. Nothing to recommend him except the ability to make things grow. Me, for instance. Asa and Marina never let me forget it."

"Didn't they treat you well?"

"They tolerated me."

"Tolerated." The word sours in my mouth.

"And they made good use of me." She flutters her hand. "It turned out well, though. They finally put me to use taking care of *you*. That made it all right."

"It doesn't sound all right to me."

"It was, though. You were my ray of sunshine. But this is old history. You must be starved. Let's see if we can't find you something to eat."

It's true, I haven't eaten since breakfast, and not much then. She rummages in the cupboard and locates a tin of fish and a stale roll, which she serves on a wooden plate.

"That's not enough," she says, watching me. "I'll run down to the kitchen. Mrs. Quay will have something to tide you over."

"For you, too?"

"Well," she says slowly, "I do enjoy those currant scones of hers."

Pouring me a cup of the tea she likes so much, my just-discovered aunt pats my head and crinkles her face in a smile. "I'll be back as soon as I can."

I watch her go, then lock the locks and curl up on the couch to wait. A thick candle squats on the mantel, throwing a wavering light on the lower part of the painting: the dog's nose, a girl's foot. I can't stop thinking about it. That painting has to be painful to look at. Why does she keep it?

Marina: slim, beautiful, graced with magic.

Edna: thick, homely, clumsy, no magic at all.

And they "put her to use."

I bite into a kipper and tear off a corner of the roll. A sip of chamomile helps them go down. Odd, the tea's in a wooden mug, quite plain. All her dishes are of wood.

An unusual person, my Aunt Edna.

Restless, I get up and wander the rooms. I don't expect to find any clues about Mother, but it can't hurt to look. Miss P. is certainly a reader, to judge by the books piled by her narrow bed—dictionaries and histories and fat old novels.

All those words! I'm reminded of the experiment Uncle Asa didn't get around to doing: making words appear on a blank page. Precipitation, he called it. Mother could do it. Can I?

I take a sheet of paper from the side table and sit down before it. What should I say? Something simple. Like this: *Mother, where are you?*

I concentrate on the phrase, each word of it, and direct my mind to the page, eyes closed tight.

Motherwhereareyoumotherwhereareyoumotherwhereareyou

I open my eyes.

Blank as a snowy field. Why did I think I could do this? I did think so. This was the one experiment I felt I could succeed at.

Try again. Slow down this time. Sink deeper. Visualize each letter as it curls into the next.

Mother. Where. Are. You?

Finally, after an endless time, I let my eyes open.

My breath catches.

In a careless script that I recognize immediately, a single, terrifying word:

Nearby.

My eyes scissor around the room. Shadows and silence. I stare at the paper, but the word remains. Is it possible? Is this a trick my mind is playing on itself? My mind's been playing all kinds of tricks lately, whenever I'm in Mother's rooms. I've had thoughts . . . feelings . . . that I don't understand. That I don't want to understand.

But Mother *nearby*? The thought should be reassuring, shouldn't it? Cause for rejoicing?

Why does it scare me so much?

I get up and head out to the sitting room, just to do something, to shake the feeling. All those locks on Miss Porlock's door—useless.

I flop down on the sofa, roll my neck around to get rid of the cricks, then reach into my bundle and take out my hairbrush. Where's a mirror? I try the bedroom. The bathroom. I look everywhere. There's not a single mirror in the place! How does Miss P. get herself made up in the morning?

Maybe she doesn't want to look at herself.

A sad thought. The more I think about it, the sadder it is.

I fetch a blanket and curl up. I'm tired—exhausted, really—but can't rest. Maybe this tea will calm me down.

A sudden knocking. I lurch from the couch. Miss Porlock! Oh, thank goodness! I hope she's brought something good.

I snap open the locks and pull the door wide.

Janko!

Janko *smiling*!

Chapter Thirty-Five

I slam the door closed. He slams it back open, knocking me off my feet. Janko's fast for someone his size. In a moment, he has me by my arm, yanks me up—*"Ow!"*—thumps me onto his shoulder, and heads down the hall, while I pound his back with my fists.

"Help! Somebody!"

Servants poke their faces out of doorways. In the back of my brain, I remember Miss Porlock saying they're all spies for my uncle. One of them probably told him where I was.

Janko starts up the spiral staircase. I'm squirming so hard I manage to knock my head against the wall. Then we're on the parapet, and cold rain hits my face. A door opens to a stink of chemicals.

Janko slings me onto the worktable, where I manage

to bang my head again. Looking up, I see Asa sharpening a knife.

"No!"

He gives me an irritated glance and goes about his business, holding the blade over a flame, while Janko pins me down.

Asa approaches. The blade glints.

"Hey!" I shout. "HEY!"

Click-click, click-click goes my glass thumb.

"Calm down!" he says.

Calm down? A bubble of hysteria rises in my throat.

"This won't hurt for long."

Oh my God, he's going to do it! I thrash about wildly and manage to land a kick to his side.

"Can't you *hold* her?" he snaps.

"She's crazy! Like holding a snake!"

Asa turns and reaches into his cabinet for a small bottle. He pulls out a handkerchief and sprinkles some liquid onto it. A sickly sweet smell makes my nose twitch.

"Hold her now!"

He presses the wet cloth to my face. I shake my head violently, but Asa's grip is tight. It's hard to think with my heart pounding like this. The heel of his hand muffles my scream.

What was I screaming about again?

Focus! Fight it!

I roll side to side, feeling for the edge of the table. I find it and get halfway off before strong hands grab my ankles and pull me back.

Somebody's struggling.

Oh yes, that girl down there.

But my body's so light! Am I floating? Never knew I could do this. Why haven't I done this before?

Up ahead stands a white door. No house, no walls, just white against white. I step through.

Behind it, a white throne. Who's supposed to sit there?

In the center of the seat, amid all the whiteness, is a tiny black spot, like a period on a page.

Look closer. It's moving!

With a shudder, I back away. It's an *insect*! Glistening black, with tiny pincers, tiny antennae testing the air.

I step farther away, keeping an eye on the insidious bug, afraid to turn my back.

My back. Actually, my hip. Something's poking me. I notice strange smells, part sweet, part sulfuric.

The throne is gone. My hip hurts. My eyes open to a blur.

Dizziness rises through me, and I swing to the side as my stomach lurches. I hear a splattering sound and smell something bad. I wipe my mouth with the back of my wrist.

Asa's laboratory! What am I doing, lying on the table like one of his specimens?

Oh, that's right. I *am* one of his specimens.

And I've just thrown up.

There he is at the end of the table, glaring at me. "Now look what you've done!"

I remember more now. "I thought . . ."

"You thought what?"

"You were going to kill me."

He looks at me in surprise. "Now, why would I do that?"

"You know. For my golden blood."

"That's an unusual expression. Where did you learn it?"

I clear my throat and wipe my mouth. "Miss Porlock told me. She said you needed my blood for your rose."

His frown deepens. "Should have known. Horrible, meddling woman!"

"She was only trying to help me. She's my aunt, you know. Your sister."

"Unfortunately. Is she the one who said I was going to kill you?"

I nod.

"Did she, by any chance, tell you anything else?"

I look at him blankly.

"Did she mention, for instance, how much I needed?" He holds up a test tube filled with dark red liquid. "A single test tube! Actually, I filled two, in case the first doesn't work."

"She didn't tell me that."

Why didn't she tell me that?

"No, she wouldn't," Asa continues. "She's been against me from the start. Says I don't know what I'm dealing with."

"Do you?" I raise myself on both elbows.

"Yes," he says firmly. "Horticulture."

"Well, if it was only that . . ."

"Horticulture with an added ingredient. One that, as it happens, does not require murdering my niece."

That's when I notice a small, neat bandage on my upper arm.

Oh.

"So," he says, "now that you are still among the living, do you want to help finish the experiment? It will take a few days. I was going to start tomorrow, but then I found out you were running away."

"Your spies told you?"

"My loyal servants."

I glance at the array of instruments and equipment: a crate of rare soil, the pots, vats, vials, tubes, and the rest.

"I think I'll skip this one."

"But," he says, "you were so interested."

"That was before."

He doesn't understand.

"You *attacked* me!" I climb off the table and stand before him, a little shaky. "No permission asked. No explanation given. No apology."

"You want an apology?"

"I want you to leave me alone."

"But how can you stop when we're so close to success?"

"What makes you think we're so close, when we failed all those other times?"

"Have you seen the book? It's ancient. By a famous necromancer."

"You mean, magician?"

"Magician, yes. I don't know who sent it, but I have a feeling about it. Your aunt has a feeling about it, too. Why else would she purposely mistranslate a key section, to keep me from succeeding?"

"She did that?"

"But I caught it. I went back to the text and puzzled it out. I tell you, this is going to work!"

His eyes are wild, repellent.

"Well then," I say, starting for the door, "it sounds like you have all you need." I want to make an impressive exit, but stagger and hold on to the table.

"Go ahead," he says to my back. "I don't need you."

"No," I say, turning. "You've gotten everything from me already. Thanks for not killing me."

"I would never do that. What do you take me for?"

I give him a slow look, then stumble out into the night.

It's only when I'm halfway down the stairs that I remember the pain in my hip. I reach in my back pocket and pull out a small piece of wood. I stare at it, turning it around in my hands, and smile for the first time all night.

It's Cole's turtle.

Chapter Thirty-Six

I approach warily. The door, I see, has been twisted cock-eyed. Janko was not gentle. I knock. Wait. Knock again.

"Miss Porlock?"

At the slightest push, the door swings open.

"Anybody here?"

The fat candle gives the only light in the sitting room, but it's enough to show Miss P. on the couch, hands on her lap, staring at the unlit hearth.

I stand before her. "Why did you lie to me?" I say quietly.

She doesn't answer.

"You made me think he was going to kill me, when you knew it wasn't so."

She turns toward me. "My dear girl," she says, "you

don't know what danger you're in. Your uncle doesn't, either, I'm afraid."

"But you lied to me."

"I may have exaggerated."

"*Exaggerated?* He took exactly two test tubes of blood. And there I was, screaming."

"That must not have been pleasant."

"You don't understand. I *trusted* you."

She looks at me sadly. "You still can, dear. You can trust me to save you. This experiment of his is not finished, you know."

"No, he's up there working on it."

"I'm sure he is." She looks at me intently. "He *must* not succeed."

"Why? What does it matter if he succeeds or not?"

"I don't care for your tone, Cisley."

"Well, I'm sorry, but I'm angry. Everyone tells me what to do, but no one tells me what's going on!"

"You're very young. There may be some things you *shouldn't* know."

"I'm not that young, and I know more than you think."

Miss P. gives me that sad, knowing smile of hers.

For some reason, this infuriates me. "Why are you smiling?"

"I know what you think you know, and I know what you don't."

"Oh?"

"I don't like to quarrel with you, Cisley. It hurts me to see you so angry."

It hurts me, too. "You think you know what's in my mind. Tell me."

She sighs. "For one thing, I know you found out about your father."

I nod. I didn't know she knew that. "What else?"

"And I know how you visit him without your uncle finding out."

"You do?"

"You go out through Marina's closet."

"You know about *that*?"

"I don't suppose there's much I *don't* know about this place."

I'm silent. I always thought of Miss P. as kindly, but a bit slow. Maybe she's neither. "What else?" I say.

"Lots of things. One could go on."

"What *else*?"

"Well," she says, drawing it out, "I know you've been getting a lot of bad advice lately." She pauses. "From a certain seashell."

She knows about the shell! She knows the secret way out of the castle. She knows. . . .

"You *broke* it, didn't you?" I burst out. "Don't deny it."

She smiles sadly. "I don't."

"Why would you *do* it? It was wicked!"

"The advice it was giving you was wicked."

"What advice was that?"

"Did it not tell you to help your uncle with his experiments?"

"How would you know that? Were you spying on me?"

"No need. It was obvious. That's what it *would* tell you."

I can't get over this! Miss Porlock, smashing my shell! If I can't trust her . . .

"Well," I say in a hard voice, "maybe I know a thing or two about you, too."

"Watch your tone, dear."

"I know that you're madly jealous of Mother."

Miss P. straightens up.

"In fact, you hate her, don't you? Always have."

Her cheeks wobble. "Cisley," she says mournfully, "how could you say such a cruel, untrue . . ."

I hold back. I was about to mention the stockings, the scissors, that night in Mother's bedroom, but I can't. I've hurt her enough. "Maybe it's not such a good idea," I say, "for me to stay here tonight."

Miss Porlock looks down at her hands.

"Uncle Asa won't be looking for me anymore. He's gotten what he needs."

No response. Miss Porlock keeps looking down, her hands twisting and twisting on her lap. She has begun muttering under her breath.

I'm trying hard to hate her.

I lay a hand gently on her shoulder.

She doesn't look up. Continues muttering.

I turn away.

Chapter Thirty-Seven

Back in my room, I push the window open and stick my head out, letting the night wind finger my hair and cold rain weep against my face. The rustle of distant waves relieves the silence, but when I come in again, the silence is waiting as before.

I sit down, but almost immediately get up again. Wander into the bedroom. Wander out. I suppose I could take a bath. That's where Elwyn used to live. How nice it would be to gossip with my little lobster friend, or argue with my conch shell, or giggle with Anna.

And now I've lost Miss Porlock.

I reach in my pocket and feel Cole's wooden turtle. Well, I haven't lost Cole, have I? Not yet.

And I have a father.

I should be with him, but there's a job to do first. Just

a little thing, shouldn't take but a moment: *find Mother.* That's what I'm here for.

I did catch a glimpse of her—was it yesterday?—in the mirror on her vanity. It's a place to start.

I head down the hall toward her rooms. As usual, the Mirror Maze confronts me with a wilderness of glass, but I follow my nose. This time, the scent is different, darker. When I finally reach the door and let myself in, I realize why: the white rose is dying. Of course it is. Father almost died himself; he couldn't be out at flower shops ordering fresh roses.

I wander into the bedroom and flop down on the velvet coverlet. I feel closest to Mother here. This is the softness she felt; these are the gauzy bed curtains she gazed at every candlelit evening. I'm not in some rich lady's room. I'm in a queen's chamber. And I'm her daughter. We share the same blood.

The same golden blood.

Looking through the bed curtains, I see, as in a cloud, the portrait of Mother. The gauze makes her look ghostly; I swing out of bed and stand in front of the painting itself.

I have the strangest feeling she's looking back at me. Her eyes are brilliant, with a hint of amusement, and, yes, a metallic touch of contempt. Standing before her, I can feel the same contempt. I understand it. It would take so little for me to make it my own.

But then I think of little Gwennie running with her

kite. I think of Father, so close to death, coming to life. I think of Cole.

I am not my mother.

Yes, you are, says a small voice in my head.

"No!" I say out loud.

I'm the only one who understands you, the voice continues. Secret. Insidious.

Mother's eyes bore into me. It's true. She understands me in ways that no one, not even Cole, ever could.

But maybe Cole understands a different me, a part that Mother knows nothing about and would not value if she did.

Taking a deep breath, I break free of her gaze. I don't know where to go, but as long as I'm in her lair, I hardly know what thoughts are hers and what are my own.

I love her, but I can't *be* her.

Maybe I should say that to her directly, if I can. I adjust the three-paneled mirror on the vanity so that three, six, a dozen, an endless number of Cisleys peer back at me.

Are you there, Mother?

I peer at the farthest Cisley I can be sure of. No mistaking that puzzleheaded girl for Marina Thummel. Maybe she's farther down the line than she was before, beyond my range of vision. I concentrate, staring till my eyes hurt. I adjust the mirror a dozen ways. Just me, me, me.

That's when a short dark line appears near the top of

the center panel. As I watch, it curves into a capital *D*. The same letter forms on the right and left panels. Soon a word appears!

Don't   *Don't*   *Don't*

"Don't what?"

Don't leave   *Don't leave*   *Don't leave*

I stare. There's something so sad about those two words.

These people   *These people*   *These people*
they   *they*   *they*

I wait.

they people   *they These*   *don't understand*
don't understand   *understand us*   *don't us*

"I know," I whisper.

them anymore   *need them any*   *you don't don't*

"You say I don't need them?"

You're stronger   *than stronger*   *they are*

That stops me. Am I? Am I stronger than Asa? I like that thought very much. For a moment, I feel, yes, I *am* like Mother. I'm stronger than people think. At the same time, I worry. What's wrong with her writing? The note she precipitated for Asa in Trieste was so sharp and clear. Are her abilities failing? Has she been away from her body too long?

We are rule   *are We ru*   *We rulers*
not serv   *not servants*   *not servan*

"Mother, are you all right? What's happening?"
A long pause. Then:

need to come   *I ne to come ba*   *need to come bac*

"But *how*? How can I help you?"
No words.
"Mother?"
No words.
No words.
No words.

PART FOUR

The Black Rose

Chapter Thirty-Eight

A couple of test tubes of blood was all it took to set me free.

I don't want to think about that. Actually, I don't want to think about Mother, either. I couldn't sleep last night, just sat on the window seat, curled in a blanket, staring out. The firth was invisible till nearly morning, when vague lines of whitecaps rose and disappeared and rose again. By then the rain had stopped.

But what a feeling, a few hours later, to walk past Mr. Strunk! I sauntered through the atrium and outside, just like a normal person. My confinement over.

I had missed all the good smells out here: warm sunlight on dune grass, fresh oil paint, a salt breeze off the water.

Best of all, Father's with me on the bluff, in front of

his easel. It's his first time out since the accident, and he's weak, but he wanted to come. "I'm wondering," he said when I showed up this morning, "would you mind if I did a portrait of you?"

I hope I didn't blush.

"In those other paintings," he said, "you were so far away." His eyes did that crinkly thing they do when he's on the edge of a smile. "I know just where I want to put you."

So here I am, perched on a rock, one knee up, looking back over my shoulder toward the painter. In my hand, I hold Cole's little turtle.

"Nice touch," says Father. "But you're holding it funny."

"Trying to keep my thumb away from it."

"Oh, that's right."

We share a look. Earlier, I confessed about putting a hole in his painting with my glass thumb. He was very good about it, even joked that I'd improved it.

One of the nicest things about today is that I'm not in disguise, dressed in Mother's gowns to fool my uncle. He's so wrapped up in the new experiment he doesn't care what I do anymore. I could drown in the firth, and he wouldn't look up.

Freedom doesn't feel real to me yet. I keep expecting Janko or Miss Porlock to come and bundle me back to the castle. I'm sitting here like a girl without a care—or a secret.

There's one secret I'm aching to tell: *Mother wrote to me on the mirror! She's trying to come back!* But I keep

258

that to myself. If she doesn't succeed, it will break Father's heart. Again.

Instead, I ask how he met her. What he thought of her that first time.

He looks at me around the canvas. "Point your chin down a little."

"Yes, Father." What a feeling to call him that!

"Your mother, you say?" His eyes narrow in concentration.

"Yes, what was your first impression?"

"Don't move your head."

The man is exasperating!

He lays down his brush. "I didn't like her."

I break the pose. "What!"

"I disliked her picture in the papers. I disliked the monstrous glass castle that she and her brother were building. I liked nothing about her. Are you shocked?"

"A little." I turn Cole's turtle from hand to hand, then place it beside me. "So how did you meet her?"

"I was starting to make a name in the art world. Nothing big. I've never made a living from my painting. But she saw my work and hired me to do her portrait."

"I love that picture!"

"I'm glad. It's the best portrait I've ever done, maybe because I was falling in love with her as I painted it."

"So you must have seen *something* good in her."

He gives his hat brim a thoughtful tug. "Let's say I saw something irresistible in her." Picking up his brush, he squints at the canvas, then at me, then back again.

"I bet she liked you a lot."

"Oh, I think I just wore her down. It took me six months to finish the painting."

"That long?"

"I dragged it out as long as I could."

I nod, smiling.

"By then I'd given her a ring, and she'd accepted it."

"You were going to get married?"

"And live happily ever after. Now," he says, "could we get back to business?" He lifts his hat and wipes his brow. "I don't want to spend six months on *this* one."

He glances in the direction of his bungalow. "Who's that?"

I recognize the loping walk before I make out the face. I jump up. "Hey, Cole!"

He waves and hurries. A basket sways over one shoulder.

"My mom thought you'd be getting hungry," he says, setting the wicker basket before us. He pulls out a blanket and starts unpacking sandwiches, apples, and a jar of sweet tea.

I spread out the blanket and pat it. "You've got to help us eat this."

Cole plunks down beside me and bumps against me on purpose. We trade smiles. "Nice seeing you in regular clothes," he says.

"Don't you like ball gowns?"

He makes a face.

Soon the three of us are jabbering away, trading sandwiches and quips. I pause and peer at the two of them over the crust of my chicken sandwich. *So this is happiness: Cole, Father, and Cisley on a picnic by the Firth of Before.*

It's been tugging at the back of my mind all morning, something Asa said to me. I don't think I should bring it up now, but when else? I lower my sandwich and turn to Father. "Why did you and Mother . . . ?"

"Break up?"

Cole and I wait.

"You know, grown-ups don't always stay together, even when they love each other."

"Why not?"

"It's complicated."

"Well," I say, "my uncle seems to think it's simple. He says he paid you to leave."

Father stiffens. "It's interesting," he says slowly, "that he's still saying that."

I've never seen Peter Underwood angry, his shoulders hunching. So little I know.

"Did he say anything else?" he says.

"Nothing, really."

"Tell me."

"He said you took the money and went away. 'Like a good dog,' he said."

"Like a . . . ?" He stands up and walks about, his hands in fists.

"Not that I believe him," I add quickly. *I don't believe him, do I?*

Father comes back. "He really said that?"

I nod.

"Well." He rubs his chin. "I suppose he's half right."

"What! You took the money?"

"No. I turned down the money. But I did leave."

"Why?"

Father sighs. "I had to face the obvious. Can you imagine Marina Thummel moving in with a penniless painter? Your *mother*? She'd have been miserable. As miserable as I'd be moving into that glass monstrosity of hers."

"I know what you mean about the castle. I like your place."

"She'd have hated it. She'd have hated me."

"I thought she hated you anyway."

He throws me an appraising look. "You're too smart for thirteen. Yes, she did hate me, because she believed Asa's story. I couldn't convince her otherwise." He sits back down and balls up the paper from his sandwich. "Of course, I had no idea *you* were in the picture."

"But she agreed to meet you on the boat."

"That's right. She sent me a letter saying she'd found out about Asa's lie. She said he laughed about it, and she was going to make him suffer."

The three of us fall silent. I don't feel hungry anymore. Our perfect little gathering—encircling an absence.

"Wait!" I say, standing up. "Do you smell something?"

Cole and Father look puzzled.

"Seaweed?" says Father.

"Chicken sandwich," says Cole.

I close my eyes. The scent is faint . . . a dark floral, with a trace of bitterness that makes my nostrils flare. It's coming from the direction of the castle.

"It's happening!" I cry.

"What?" Cole says. He, too, stands up.

"No, you stay here. I need to do this by myself."

"Do what? What's happening?"

"The rose!" I start off at a run. "He's made the rose!"

Chapter Thirty-Nine

Out of breath, I stumble through the atrium. The smell is stronger here, a cloying sweetness with an acrid undertone, but Strunk seems unaware of it.

"Miss Thummel, are you quite all right?"

"Don't you smell it?"

"Excuse me?"

"The smell, Mr. Strunk, the smell!"

The little man looks around, as if smells might be visible. His feathery eyebrows twitch. "Nothing out of the ordinary."

These last words are spoken to my back, because I'm running now. I take the glass staircase two steps at a time, reach the landing, then rabbit past my rooms to the spiral stairs. As I reach the roof, the smell grows stronger and stranger by the second.

It can only be the rose!

He's done it!

Sunlight bounces off the glass turrets as I fling open the door to the laboratory. The scent overwhelms me—not the sweetness of fresh blossoms, but the sweetness of decay, as if I've opened a long-sealed tomb. In the center of it stands my wild-eyed uncle.

I run to him, no word spoken, and watch what he's watching: an apparatus of glass-and-rubber tubing, in the center of which stands a blood-red rose (red with *my* blood, I realize). I start to say something, but Asa holds up a finger. Within a minute, the rose begins to darken. Cranberry deepens to maroon, dims to burgundy, then eggplant, then . . .

Midnight!

All the while, the scent grows stronger, dizzying. Asa laughs, a low rumble that erupts in a bark. I feel a little light-headed myself.

As we stare, the rose, now completely black, continues to change. It's not any less black. If possible, its blackness has reached an even darker depth—but the petals are thinning. In fact, they've grown practically transparent. I can see through to the bright leaves behind.

"I did it!" Asa's voice is hoarse.

I'm transfixed. He was right after all. Weeks ago, he told me that black is not a color, but an absence—that a pure black rose would be invisible. The blossom before us is now a trace of itself. Step back, and you'd believe the plant was all leaves, with no flower at all.

The smell, though, is powerful, the sweetness nauseating. I crook my arm over my nose and breathe as lightly as I can.

Asa, though, bends over the invisible flower and breathes in deeply.

The words from Mother's letter come back to me: *Inhale the scent of a pure black rose.*

His body flinches, but he leans in again and inhales more deeply than before. When he straightens, his face is flushed, his eyes bleary. "Aah!"

His sigh turns into a giggle. He totters around the room, hilarity subsiding, then breaking out again. He's drunk. Or is it just that I've never seen him happy before? Is it possible that, in his whole life, my uncle has never been happy?

He faces me, his eyes challenging. "Well, Miss Cisley, what do you say? A bit of magic?"

He squares himself in front of the fat Latin book, his brows lowered in concentration.

"Rise!"

The book does a little fidget on the table, then lies still.

"Rise! I command you!"

The book's front cover lifts an inch or two and settles back.

He frowns at me. "What am I doing wrong?"

I want to stay out of this. He is not a person I want to encourage.

"What should I do? *Tell* me!"

"I don't know, Uncle Asa. I feel things best through my hands."

"Your hands?"

All right, I can say this much. "Maybe if you hold them out?"

He extends his arms, his fingers stiff as prongs. *"Rise, book!"*

Slowly, almost lazily, the heavy volume floats upward and wobbles several feet over the table.

"Ha, ha!" he shouts. At which point, the book slams down again. "I *did* it!" He stares at me as his witness. "By God, Cisley! You saw it!"

I nod weakly. It's about all I can do. A wave of dizziness sweeps over me, and I touch my fingers to my forehead. "Uncle Asa, I think we need to get out of here."

"Leave *now*?" His eyes are dilated, his nose running with mucus. "Just when I'm doing real magic? You saw, didn't you? There were no mirrors, were there? No mirrors!" He breaks out in a peal of laughter.

"Got to get some air!" Gagging, I stumble to the door and barely make it outside before I collapse on the glass tiles and throw up. I lie there, breathing hard, then throw up some more. I groan and struggle to my feet. The breeze is cool. I take deep gulps of air and lean against the wall, looking out over the firth to steady myself.

A crash from inside! *What now?* I rush back in, covering my face with my sleeve. A spotted lizard floats past my head. The air is filled with strange things—a glass vial,

267

calipers, books, a terrified mouse, several flowerpots—all dancing overhead. Several less fortunate objects lie broken on the floor.

Asa howls with laughter, his arms outstretched as if conducting an orchestra.

"Uncle Asa!"

A measuring cup floats toward me, and I pluck it from the air. Asa turns in circles. A metal bowl falls and clangs at his feet.

"*Uncle Asa! Stop!*"

This isn't happiness. It's delirium. I breathe through my sleeve as lightly as I can, but my stomach is rising again.

"*Uncle Asa! The air is poisonous!*"

He's not listening. I take the measuring cup and throw it at him, hitting his shoulder. He looks over at me and breaks into a loopy grin. "I did it, Cisley, old girl. I don't need her. I don't need *anyone!*"

With that, he twirls around again, then stops, looks off to the right as if struck by an odd thought. A moment later, his knees buckle and he collapses on the floor.

There are thuds and crashes on all sides. A small hammer bounces off my shoulder. A spoon, then a mouse, land on my back. All his magic tricks are raining down.

I run to him, brush aside broken glass, and hold his head. His eyes! He's bleeding from his eyes!

"Uncle Asa!"

More crashes. *Got to get him outside!*

I attempt to lift him, but he's heavy.

A dead weight.

Dead.

Desperate, I grab his ankles and try to drag him. I back into the worktable and have to pull him the other way.

"Don't worry, Uncle Asa. I'll get you out of here!"

"Nice of you."

My head snaps up. *A woman's voice?*

I scan the laboratory. No one. Wait: there, across the room, a shimmer. I watch, terrified, as it narrows into the shape of a woman . . . tall, in a pale blue gown. . . .

"Mother?"

The woman looks at me for long seconds, her body moving in and out of focus. "Hello, dear."

I'm too stunned to move, fear mixing with disbelief, disbelief with tears. I take a step toward her. She holds up a hand. "Wait! I'm not here yet."

Not here? Everything's a blur to my streaming eyes. I can hardly tell what's here and what isn't. It's especially hard with my head banging with pain and my stomach lurching.

"Soon," she coos, "soon." Then she adds: "Thanks to you."

"To me?"

She nods slowly, as if testing out what she can do in this not-quite body. "Without you," she says, "there would be no rose. I used to have the mirror to get back and forth, but after it broke, the rose was the only way."

"I don't understand." My glass thumb has started

clicking. I concentrate to make it stop. Now if I could stop the dizziness.

"The rose made an opening. It's half in this world, half in the other." Her smile is a sliver of light. "You didn't want to help him," she says. "I had to keep after you."

"You did?" I hold on to the worktable for support.

"I was talking to you all the time. You didn't know that?"

I ransack my memory. When did she talk to me?

"It wasn't easy," she goes on. "That creature had a mind of his own. Take my advice, dear. Never try to talk through a lobster. Always interjecting his own thoughts. The shell was so much easier."

"Wait." I grope to understand.

"My dear," says Mother with a pretty frown, "here I am going on about myself. Shouldn't we get you some air?"

"Shouldn't we?" I can't keep track of who shouldn't or what shouldn't. It hardly matters, because I lose my hold on the table and slide to the floor. The cement is cool against my cheek.

"Oh," I hear above me, "that wasn't supposed to happen."

A gust of wind blows in, a door slams, and then another voice, harsh: "*What* wasn't supposed to happen, Marina? What's that horrible smell?"

"Don't you like roses?"

Someone's bending over me. I smell the body powder of Miss Porlock.

"Marina," I hear her say, "what have you done? Come, Cisley, I'm getting you out of here."

"Yes, take her out, Edna. I'd help, but as you see, I'm not myself."

Sounds of voices, back and forth. Someone is angry. At least I can breathe better, this close to the floor. An arm slides under my shoulder, but Miss Porlock isn't strong enough to lift me. She takes me by the legs and starts dragging me.

Then stops. "Dear God!" she cries. "What have you done to Asa?"

Mother's voice, just as sharp: "Nothing you wouldn't have done, given the chance. You hate him more than I do."

"Hate Asa? He's our brother!"

"Yes, and I'm your sister. Look what you did to me!"

"Marina! How can you think—?"

"Don't deny it. We all know about your gift. The one pathetic bit of magic you have. Breaking things! Mirrors, especially. It *was* you, wasn't it?"

"I don't have to answer that."

"I *knew* it was you! It was a *horrible* thing you did, trapping me in there for months."

"No more than you deserved. Wait. There's no pulse! You *killed* him!"

"Did I? Oh. Maybe so."

"You killed our brother!"

"I just wanted to torment him a little. Get back at him. Like when I pricked my finger before the magic show and dripped blood on the scarf. A bit of fun, that's all."

"Fun! Come on, Cisley."

"Yes, take her outside," calls Mother's echoey voice. "Another minute is all I need. Then I'll take over."

"You'll have nothing to *do* with her!"

Mother's laughter is a silver waterfall. "Is *that* what this is about, Edna? You want her for yourself? Is *that* why you broke the mirror? To keep me from taking her away?"

Silence.

"That's it, isn't it?"

Silence.

"Oh, Edna, Edna. You think she loves you?" More silver laughter. "Look at yourself in the mirror sometime, you ridiculous woman!"

"Quiet!"

"You poor, deluded—"

"Quiet, I said!"

Mother's laughter echoes through the building.

A sudden, violent crash of glass, and then a howl such as I've never heard from any creature, animal or human. It's Mother!

I lift my head from the floor, just enough to see my mother, her face a contortion of horror as she's sucked into the distance. Back into the invisible!

"Mother!" I croak. *"No!"*

A much louder crash now. Then others, close and far away.

A moment later, something warm and heavy falls on top of me, knocking me windless.

I can scarcely breathe under the heavy weight. The smell of body powder and perfume mingles with the stink of the rose. I blink my eyes hard and try to focus. In front of me on the glass-strewn floor lies a mangled rosebush amid spilled dirt and rubber tubing.

The sight of it fascinates me. I catch what breath I can and watch. The faint outline of a blossom takes form.

The outline fills in. Darkens.

Black petals! How beautiful!

The changes continue. Black saddens to almost black. Brownish red now. Then dirty brown.

As I watch, hypnotized, the petals curl inward and shrivel. From the broken stem, reddish fluid slowly drips.

The rose is dying.

It's all right; I'm dying, too.

Mother's dying. Porlock. Asa.

We'll die together.

Chapter Forty

Leave me alone.

Someone's pulling at me. Interfering. And here I was sinking so nicely. The blackness of blackness, darkest velvet.

Stop it!

I feel lighter suddenly. A great weight off me. Oh, that's better!

Someone's arm under my shoulder, then under my knees. I'm being lifted.

"Cisley, wake up!"

Nice voice.

"Cis! Come on. I can't lose you."

Lose me? I'm right here.

"Cisley!"

I force my eyes open a sliver. Cole! I try to say something, but my throat is clogged.

"Stay with me, Cis!"

Sure, I'll stay with you. I love you, Cole Havens. Do you know that?

Bang! I jump at the noise. A slice of glass sticks in the counter next to us and quivers like a thrown knife. Another shard hurtles down nearby, spattering bright splinters.

"Gotta get out!" Cole shouts, heading toward the door, or where it used to be. Half the wall is missing.

As he steps out, I glance behind me.

"Don't look!" he says, swiveling so I can't see.

But I do.

Oh God, I see! A lump of a woman facedown on the floor, daggers of glass jutting from her flowered dress, her back oozing.

"Is that . . . ?" My voice sounds like gargling. I twist around as Cole carries me.

"Never mind!" he says.

"No! Stop!" I croak. The sight of my old tutor focuses my mind. "Let me down!"

"There's nothing you can do," he says, but eases me onto my feet.

A breeze coming through the broken panes carries away the fumes, and with a steadier head, I see Miss Porlock clearly. I work my way toward her, leaning for support on the worktable while glass continues shattering all around us.

I hadn't noticed till now a man's body sprawled nearby at an unnatural angle. *Asa!* His face is a mangle of glass and blood, eyes staring sightlessly. My own eyes can't meet his for long. I know he's gone. I'm not sure about Miss Porlock.

Those horrible shards of glass! I don't know whether to pull them out or . . . ?

As I kneel beside her, more glass drops from the ceiling and shatters.

"We can't stay, Cisley."

"Wait! No!" I place my hands carefully on Miss Porlock's back and try to concentrate. I can usually feel a person's life—how much of it there is—through my hands. All I feel is the unnatural coolness of her body.

I lift her wrist and feel for a pulse. Nothing.

A gasp from Cole. He's holding his upper arm.

"What is it? *Are you cut?*"

He nods, wincing.

"Oh, Cole!" I'm up on my feet and stumbling out to the patio, Cole beside me.

Stopping by the turret, I have him show me the cut. Not as bad as I feared. He rolls his sleeve to his shoulder, and I grasp the wound tightly, bending my head in concentration.

"Cis, we don't have time."

"Don't speak." I close my eyes tight, and before long feel the familiar warmth building in my hands. But there's something else. I can't tell if he's trembling or if I am. It's the merest vibration, but it quickly gets stronger.

I open my eyes. He's looking at the laboratory, what's left of it, and there's fear in his eyes. I follow his gaze as one of the larger panes crashes to the ground.

"This whole place could come down!" he cries. "Can you walk?"

"I think so." At least his arm looks better, bleeding just slightly.

Another crash sends us running for the staircase. The next floor down, a chambermaid calls to the young valet. I can't make out the words. All I hear is her panic.

Someone flies past us along the corridor. Then others. I hear a deep groaning sound, like the sound a ship might make in heavy seas. A tremendous *boom* jolts me, and I hold tightly to Cole's waist. We're in a stumbling run, making for the main staircase. Not far ahead, a chandelier plummets to the floor, exploding like a bomb.

"Hurry!" I shout.

We pass my rooms and arrive at the curving staircase. The valet is already halfway down, gripping the hand of the terrified chambermaid. As we start to follow, a deep rumbling rises from below, and suddenly a whole section of the staircase separates from the wall. Desperate, the man grapples for the railing, but it isn't attached to anything!

Near the top, the stairs swing to the side, and Cole loses his balance, his arms flailing. I catch hold of his belt as he starts to fall, but I'm still weak and am nearly pulled after him.

"No!" I snarl through gritted teeth, my arms trembling,

feet braced against the side of the staircase. *"No, sir! Not today!"*

I don't know how I manage to drag him back to the landing just as the whole staircase crashes to the atrium below with a force that shakes the building. A great cloud rises toward us, glinting with silica.

Cole sits on the landing, dazed, his feet dangling over nothingness.

Below us, I hear an old man's cough, and then, through the confusion of debris, I catch sight of Mr. Strunk stumbling through the atrium.

"Run, Mr. Strunk!"

He doesn't hear me.

"How can we get down?" Cole struggles to his feet and backs away from the edge.

I'm not used to seeing fear in his eyes. It disturbs me. "I know a way."

"Another staircase?"

"Mother's room." I tug his shirt. "Quick!"

Not that I can do anything quickly. With my arm around his shoulder, we hobble in the direction of the Mirror Maze. There it lies just ahead, glittering and deadly.

"Wait!" The image of Miss Porlock's bloody body flashes through my mind. "It's too dangerous."

"There's no way around," says Cole.

A pounding of heavy feet makes us turn. It's Janko, bleeding from his cheek, his eyes wide.

"Don't go through there, Janko!"

He shoves me aside with a force that knocks me off my feet, and then plunges into the maze. Cole holds me against his chest to keep me from seeing, but I can't help myself. Three, then seven Jankos, having no clue where to go, slam into mirrors, jarring the already shaky structure. Twelve Jankos flail their bleeding arms and roar as the Mirror Maze turns into an avalanche of knives.

Then begins a dreadful subtraction. With mirrors falling, fewer Jankos remain. They stagger helplessly.

Eight Jankos.

Five.

Four Jankos clutch their necks as glass stilettos slice at them. They thrash about, knocking into remaining mirrors.

Two Jankos hold a stunned pose, arms raised. Then, together, they topple facedown in a pile of glass.

My stomach churns. I grip Cole's hand.

Gingerly, no word spoken, we step into the maze, no longer a maze. Avoiding Janko's torn body, we pick our way along, shards crunching under our feet.

Soon we're in front of Mother's door.

I push it open.

Relief! The rooms have been spared, their silence intact. Even the white rose, shriveled as it is, stands on the mantel. My shoulders relax. The velvet coverlet purrs, and I want to crawl under it.

A faint tinkling makes me glance up, where a trickle of ground glass sifts from the ceiling and flitters through the bed's canopy.

Cole and I stare at each other. A small bottle of perfume chatters across the vanity. Mother's silver-backed hairbrush dances off the edge and bumps to the floor. Slowly, a ceiling crack widens, and soon chunks of plaster and glass begin to tumble through. One jagged piece, the size of a scimitar, slashes diagonally across the portrait of Mother, leaving a wide flap, like skin, hanging down.

"*Oh!*" I cry out.

"Let's go!" Cole shouts above the rising clamor. "Where are those stairs you talked about?"

I'm frozen in front of the painting.

"Cisley! *Come on!*"

I hear the roar out in the corridor, behind the walls, under my feet.

"Mother!" I call hopelessly.

"What? Where? You mean the painting?"

I lost her in the laboratory—that terrible scream still echoes—and now this!

Cole tugs my arm. "Come now!"

A tear works down my cheek.

Cole holds my shoulders and makes me look at him. I take a shaky breath. "Yes. This way." I lead him to the closet.

Once inside, there's hostility in the air. The dresses are hissing! So different from the seductive murmurings of my earlier visits. *Hissing!* They hate me. They blame me!

I stumble on until we reach the full-length mirror

at the back of the closet. A crack runs crazily down its whole length. I place my hand over the split heart of my reflection, and the mirror slides aside.

The light's dimmer here, but we keep moving, feeling our way. Before long, the floor tilts sharply downward.

"Sit down," I tell Cole.

He looks at me strangely but does what I say. I sit behind him, holding on tight, and we begin to slide, slowly at first, then faster, streaking through the darkness. We bump to a stop, and I struggle up, feeling for the door I know is in front of me. I find it and push.

Blinding daylight. *Deafening* daylight, for immediately a great roaring engulfs us. At first, I think it's the ocean, then realize it's coming from behind us, loud as a speeding train.

"Run!" I yell.

We scramble down the rocks and reach the beach, Cole helping me along when I stumble. "Keep going!" he shouts over the increasing racket.

Up ahead, the fishing boats float at anchor, as if this were just another summer day. But the men, a crowd of them, stand silently by their skiffs, staring at the castle.

I stop and look back, shocked at the sight of crumbling turrets, great blocks of glass smashing through the roof and what remains of the laboratory. It flashes through my mind that my uncle's up there and Miss Porlock— and somewhere, in some unknown form, Mother! Guilt almost knocks me to my knees; but there's no time for it. The castle's west face is trembling.

"It's coming down!" Cole shouts.

It doesn't. Everything gets quiet. Breathless. I'm barely breathing myself.

Then a terrible groan rises from the depths, as girders twist in on themselves, and the great castle, glittering like the sun itself in the afternoon light, tilts toward the sea. Tilts farther. Hesitates. At last, in a slow-motion explosion of brilliance, it topples, thundering to the rocks below, sending fiery splinters slashing through the air.

Cole and I hold on to each other, stunned. We watch as a huge cloud of debris billows upward, higher than the cliffs, then gradually subsides, settling over the dunes, over the rocks, over the vast, indifferent sea.

Chapter Forty-One

The next minutes are chaos—people running past, some bleeding, some covered in sand and dust. A housemaid I recognize—a woman in her fifties—stumbles into the open, her dress in shreds, and collapses.

I feel Cole grip my arm, but I twist free and run to her. Blood is leaking from the woman's mouth and from deep gouges in her back and hips. Too late! But still, I kneel and position my hands around the worst of the wounds. No response. My abilities do not include raising the dead. I let Cole pull me to my feet.

"It's my fault."

"What?" he says. "What do you mean?"

Windblown dirt sends me into a fit of coughing. "My fault. All of this."

He takes me by my shoulders. "Cisley, this is *not* your *fault*."

I look down at the dead woman. "What did she know about roses?"

"Cis, it was your *uncle*."

Cole can say that, but this person would be alive if it weren't for me. I made the rose possible. Look at my hands. Red and sticky.

Repulsed, I run into the water and wash them, rubbing hard as if to reverse it all.

A familiar figure staggers past. "Mr. Strunk!" I call out. He doesn't hear.

"Mr. Strunk! Wait!" I run over and stop him. He stares as if he's never seen me before. There are nasty-looking cuts on his shoulder and upper leg. "Mr. Strunk, sit down! Let me look at you!"

He always told me exactly what to do and not to do; but now he looks like a bewildered child. He sits.

Where to begin? Start with the worst. I lay my hands on his leg, where the pants have been slashed and a gash bleeds freely. Amid the tumult of shouts and the thudding of running feet, I close my eyes and sink into myself. Soon, warmth builds in my palms. Strunk twitches.

"Easy," I murmur. "It's going to be all right."

My hands grow hot. Strunk moans.

I give it another full minute, then a few seconds more, ignoring the madness around us. Carefully, I lift my hands. A red line zigzags across his upper thigh. The wound is almost closed.

Cole is coughing and trying to speak at the same time. His face wavers above me.

"Are you okay?" he says. "Because you're swaying."

I do feel dizzy, but the gash on Strunk's shoulder is as bad as the other was. Gently, I lay my hands over it.

It takes all my concentration. Again, my hands grow warm, then hot, and the bleeding slows. I'm so drained I can't think straight. When Cole helps me to my feet, I lean heavily against him.

"I can't leave yet."

"You've done enough."

I look down the beach. "Wait! Who's that?"

A dark-skinned boy, shirtless and bleeding, sits cross-legged on the sand. A foot-long length of wood, part of a shattered pole, protrudes from his chest, just below the shoulder.

Cole shouts: "Nicolae!"

The boy doesn't look up.

Cole kneels. "Nicolae, look at me!"

The Gypsy boy lifts his head lazily, his eyes vague.

I shake myself alert. "Cole," I say, "sit behind him. Let him lean into your lap."

He looks at me. Nods. Gently pulls his friend back onto his lap.

"Good. Hold his head. I can't have him moving around when I do this."

Cole holds the boy's head.

I don't give myself time to think. Kneeling beside the

boy, I grab hold of the stake and—gritting my teeth—yank it out of him and fling it aside.

Nicolae stares at me, his mouth open in an amazement of pain.

I immediately press my hand, then both hands, against the wound. It's pulsing, but I won't let it bleed.

Now, I tell myself, closing my eyes. *Let's heal this boy.*

It's bad. I won't think how bad, or how weak I feel. *We can do this, Nicolae. I'm not going to lose you. I'm not!*

I sink deep, deeper, until Cisley and Nicolae are no longer anywhere, just give and take, warm and warm, a flow. Don't release him yet! The bleeding is deep. Muscle and nerve. He needs more time.

But how can I . . . ?

I know I've fainted when I feel hands lifting me up. I open a bleary eye. It's Anna! I smile weakly. Lifting my head, I see she's here with her little brother, Hanzi. Nicolae lies unconscious, his wound oozing.

"Not finished," I say, struggling to get up.

"Is all right," says Anna. "We take him now."

Cole helps me to my feet, but has to catch me as my knees give way.

He hoists me onto his shoulder and starts along the beach. But he's just a boy, and, after a dozen steps, has to put me down.

"I'll take her." A different voice. Male. Older. I'm being lifted. I rest my head against the man's shoulder.

Oil paint.

Then blackness.

Chapter Forty-Two

Two weeks make such a difference. Getting to sleep is still not easy, and when I do drift off, I lurch awake with the echo of Mother's scream in my ears. I shudder at the bitterness in that cry as she's sucked into the astral world. After that, sleep isn't likely, and I end up under the stars, listening to the sea.

But Father is a great encourager. Work helps, too. We're building a new wing on his cottage. A room of my own!

"What do you think?" he says, looking down from his perch on the ladder. "Is it beginning to look like something?"

It's beginning to look like a child's playhouse—built by a child—but I don't say that. I hand up the bucket of nails, and Father takes two, holding one between his teeth, pounding the other into the ledger board. Neither of us knows much about carpentry, but with Cole's help, we've made a start.

"Why don't you have some more tea?" Father says.

I make a face.

"It'll build up your strength."

It's true; whatever Anna's mother put in it, the *meski* has helped. I'm pretty much recovered from the poisonous rose. Not at all recovered from what happened.

Father catches my expression. "What's wrong?"

"I'm fine!" My voice is a little too bright. He climbs down.

I glance aside a moment before meeting his eyes. "Couldn't I have saved more of them?"

I can see he's looking for something positive to say. "You saved that Gypsy boy. And Strunk."

"That's true."

"And now Strunk wants to help."

I nod. "I need someone like him. What do I know about—anything?"

"You'll learn. You're the heir to the Thummel fortune now."

"What's left of it."

"Well, there's the glass factory."

"About which I know nothing."

"Strunk's good at details. He's working on hiring back the Gypsies your uncle fired. I think he'd do anything you ask."

We lapse into silence, the silence of those who have

lost everything. There's been no sign of Mother since that day, no way for her to come back after the rose was destroyed and the book of instructions lost.

I examine the lines in Father's face. They're deeper than they were a few weeks ago. "This has been hard on you," I say.

He gives my shoulder a squeeze. "I've learned something, being around you. Don't look at me that way. I have."

I have to smile. "What have you learned?"

"That some people are givers and some people are takers."

"I'm nothing."

He shakes his head. "You can't believe that." He glances out at the firth. "Marina? She could do wonderful things, dazzling things. But I wonder . . ."

I look at him.

"I wonder if she could have done what you did."

I want to say yes, of course. The truth is, I've never seen her do anything but magic tricks and practical jokes. At a party once, she proposed a toast, and then raised her glass without actually touching it. Another time, her brother was reading a book and she made the pages go blank. Did she ever use her power to help anyone?

"I guess I don't know," I say finally.

Father watches me closely. "Looking at you," he says, "I don't see her kind of ability. I don't think you do magic, Cisley."

"You don't?"

"No." He pauses. "You do miracles."

The breath catches in my chest. No one has ever said such a thing or thought such a thing.

"You don't have to believe it," he says, "but I see it."

I turn away. I can't look at Father right now. He's wrong, of course. I lift the mug and take a swallow of the terrible tea.

"I think I'll take a little walk," I say, "if you don't need me."

I clamber down the bluff to the beach, then continue on, grateful for the wind ruffling my hair, and the slap and suck of the tide. Without thinking, I head toward the castle. Or where it was. I haven't been there since the disaster, but I need to go back. I pass the docks and follow the shore till the cliff rises before me. So strange to look up and see nothing! Like running your tongue over the place where a tooth used to be.

Miss Porlock turned the Crystal Castle into a sand castle. Did she intend to? She must have had more magic than anyone thought, and she wasn't good at controlling it. I remember that afternoon at the tea shop when her cup broke and hot tea spilled over her dress. Now that I think of it, she kept no mirrors, no glass of any kind—only wood—in her rooms. I guess she didn't trust herself.

I always thought there was something false about the castle, with all those trick mirrors, but I'll miss walking along the seawall, looking out at the town and shore.

There's the boulder Cole hid behind when I first met him. It's buried in sand now. And there's where I used to sit with Elwyn.

Listlessly, I wade in the shallows, letting wavelets sweep around my ankles. Cold water, hot summer sun, endless blue sky. Reaching a rocky jag in the shoreline, I peer into the tidal pools, with their waving anemones and seaweed.

In one of them, just now, a stray sunbeam picks out a glint of gold.

Gold?

I look closer. My heart jumps. There's a lobster down there. A lobster with a golden collar!

"Elwyn!" I plunge my hand in the water to grab the creature and pull him out dripping, his many legs flailing. "You're back!"

I place him on a large rock and gaze at him lovingly. I don't notice any particular love in his tiny eyes, but then, I startled him.

"What have you been doing? You must have had great adventures!"

He starts crawling down the side of the rock, heading for the water. I pick him up and set him back on the stone.

"Elwyn! It's me, Cisley. Remember me?"

He starts off down the side of the rock. I set him back on top.

"No, you don't! Not till you talk to me!" I hold him there. I remember now what Mother told me. She said she'd been speaking to me through Elwyn. Some of the time anyway.

My voice falters. "Mother?"

No response.

"Mother, are you there?"

The lobster struggles to get free.

"Say something!"

No spark of recognition. The Elwyn I knew is not there.

Mother is not there.

Lobsters can't talk.

That fact has been obvious to everyone but me. Elwyn is a lobster. Lobsters can't talk.

This is too hard.

"All right," I say, taking my hand away, "go if you want to."

The lobster stays where he is for some seconds, then slowly moves down the side of the rock.

I don't believe you came back and then won't speak to me!

The creature steps into the water. His golden collar glimmers dimly in the shadows.

As I watch, it grows brighter. He climbs onto a submerged rock, and his head pokes through the surface. For several seconds, we stare at each other. Slowly, he waves a feeler. He looks at me some more. The feeler waves again. Then he backs down off his rock and disappears.

"Wait! Were you waving at *me*? Or were you just doing some lobster thing?"

I watch the water for minutes. No sign.

Sighing, I splash through the foamy wavelets. I don't know if I'm glad I've seen him or not. If Elwyn can't talk, is Mother dead?

Dead or alive, she's gone. More absent than ever. I feel like an orphan.

Then I remember I'm not.

In the distance, a seagull is soaring. But there's something odd; it's not flying the way a bird flies, but—yes!—the way a kite flies. I can just make out, far up the beach, a small figure running. Gwennie!

And now I hear a faint tapping sound. Up ahead on the bluff stands the little cabin, with two tiny figures climbing about on the roof. One is Father, hammering. The other, just starting down the ladder, Cole.

Father takes off his hat and wiggles it at me. Then Cole turns and sees me.

I wave. Something's different inside me. Something that makes me walk a little faster.

I follow the curve of the shore into my new life.

Acknowledgments

A special thanks to my Braintrust, an elite group of readers I turn to for advice; and to the Heartland Writers, who tunneled through each chapter as it was written.

I'm grateful to Grace Townley and Spencer Lott for being a sounding board; to composer Bruce Wolosoff for turning an early story into brilliant music; to my agent, Jodi Reamer, for excellent representation; to Nancy Siscoe for wise and sharp-eyed editing; and, finally, to Wyatt Townley for invaluable brainstorming and constant encouragement. I am the lobster on her golden leash.

About the Author

Roderick Townley taught in Chile on a Fulbright Fellowship, worked in New York as an editor, and now spins fantasies from his home in Kansas. Critics have called his work "beloved from the first page" (*Kirkus Reviews*, Starred), "sure to become a classic" (*VOYA*), and "brilliantly conceived, superbly written" (*Carousel*). His novels include *The Door in the Forest*, *The Blue Shoe*, *The Red Thread*, *Sky*, and the trilogy of the Sylvie Cycle: *The Great Good Thing*, *Into the Labyrinth*, and *The Constellation of Sylvie*.

He lives at the edge of the woods with his wife, the poet laureate of Kansas, Wyatt Townley. You can read more about Roderick Townley and his magical books at rodericktownley.com.